GOO

Published in the United States by Goo Factory, LLC, in Los Angeles, in 2013. First Edition.

**Goo Factory ISBN: 978-0-9912974-0-5**

Cover by Chris ONeill

www.goofactory.tv

Printed in the United States of America

*I would like to thank Lola and Pudger, for their relentless moral support in the shape of licks and snuggles; Chris ONeill, for reading my manuscript over and over again and for putting together a sexy cover; Shani Vellvé, for being the closest thing possible to an editor (without whom this entire book would be a maze of confusion); and LeeAnna Neumeyer, for showing me how to say "fuck you".*

All that we see or seem is but a dream within a dream.
**–Edgar Allan Poe**


You live in illusion and the appearance of things.
There is a reality, but you do not know this.
When you understand this, you will see that you are nothing.
And being nothing, you are everything.
That is all.
**–Kalu Rinpoche**

R³

# $\mathbf{R^3}$

*March 14th, 1592*

    *It was gone, as fast as it'd appeared. No longer
to be seen, devoured by the void. It was everything
and anything all at once. It was beautiful. I saw it
all, the end through the beginning. As a
mathematician, my initial reaction was to examine,
to deconstruct, but even as numbers, the knowledge
was ungraspable. I was ecstatic, filled with joy as
tears swelled my eyes. Yet all I did was smile. It was
the absolute, the first and the last, infinity within the*

water drop. All infinite potentials and outcomes in one.

Nothing in my life had ever prepared me for this experience. Millions of thoughts flooded my mind, instantly doubting what my every sense was experiencing. I blamed it on my lack of water; dehydrated for days. The scorching sun overpowered my weak limbs, but I knew I had a grip on my wits. This was real. Real as real can get. Tangible as tangible gets. It wasn't my tired mind playing tricks on me because I was not the only one there. Yet, I was the only one left. The thought of poison did cross my mind. A strong hallucinogen, perhaps? But I hadn't ingested anything other than what was in my pack. Another disproving option, discarded. What struck me the most, however, was what followed.

A sequence of infinite numbers flashed before me. Then merged into one. Next, lives flickered past me. They also merged into one. Past, present, future; all radiated through the one eye, the source. And that's when I knew—this was the answer.

The answer to everything, to every single question. The secret to all life and the universe.

We are all born to d—

**ONE**

## DARKNESS

I remember the dream. The vacuum.

There is no sound here, except for distinct crackles at no specific interim; sounds resembling the crushing of a paper bag or soda can.

Light-flares radiate. A pulsating aurora borealis is interweaved with a phosphorescent hexagonal grid; a path on a black canvas. Flickering firefly pixels fling endlessly, creating swarms of scintillating stardust—a fluid constant. Rapidly shifting perspective waves in and out, interlocking with each other, dissolving and falling back into place. The environment is alive, moving, breathing on its own rhythm.

A slender, shimmering, silvery object slices through the prismatic environment, shattering through the grid, leaving a trail of ripples and splintering rhombi behind. But this is not "space". This is something else. And like every journey measured with the hand of time, the metallic object passes through, unleashing chaos, yet its stay in this environment is transitory.

*Everything falls…*

*Have you dreamt before?*

**THE YEAR OF THE NOW**

I was lucky it was empty.

*What's this place anyway? How did I get here?*

As I scan through the numbers embedded on the wall of narrow doors, I realize the dilapidated storage facility could easily be a collection of PO Boxes. Unkempt, dim-lit. But it isn't. It looks more like a locker room at a correction facility.

I finally stop in front of a locker, not sure why – the number reads "314". I guess this is the one. I look around once more, but I'm still alone. All alone. Even if I weren't, who'd recognize me? I've never been here before, probably will never come back. I'm simply one more guy with a non-memorable face, which easily explains why I was doomed to a mediocre existence from the get go. Non-memorable face with an equally dull personality, bound to an average life with the bunch. I don't complain. It is what it is. It's not like I was planning on becoming President or seeking an equally pretentious celebrity status in what some people (not sure who) call (for some reason) "the biz". I consider myself attractive, in an interesting type of way, enough for a drunken fuck with a sloppy college student or the occasional hottie, but nothing long-term. That's usually how it goes and I'm content with that.

The combination came to me as easy as it was to find the right locker. I was simply (yet unexplainably) led to it. Inside sat a lonely, medium-sized, black duffel bag. There was no need to look at the contents. I already knew what was inside. *How?* Not really sure. I just did.

Bill kept pulling out more and more bottles out of his bag, choking the life out of the tiny coffee table in my tiny apartment. He's a cool guy, but I don't really know where he gets all this stuff, most of which I've never seen in my life. Perhaps that's why he's a dealer—though he would never really strike you as one, with his long, grayish hair, his pruney Chinese face and the collection of New Age necklaces and scarves wrapped around his neck and head. Shiny beads cover his bionic left arm, which you'd think would only make it look more state-of-the-art, but bionic prosthetics are as common as overweight diabetics in America. He lost his arm years ago; he avoids the subject all together. Apparently the surgery was botched, which killed most of his nerve endings.

I grab a bottle that reads *Aspirin*. "Acetylsalicylic acid?"

"The main component in Aspirin," he shoots back with a smile.

There's a hammer at arm's reach, framed by Bill's pharmaceuticals. I've never seen it before. "Is this your hammer?"

"No," he says without interrupting his pill organization.

"What does it do?" I ask while crushing the white pill with the hammer.

"Pain reliever. Very popular before the incident... Until they developed the snowflake, that is."

As if on cue, a snowflake commercial takes over my small telly. These occurrences seem to happen a lot. Random. Or luck. When do they stop being random and start becoming a pattern?

# R³

A young woman grabs her head feebly, signaling, "oh, I have a headache" in an obviously pathetic way – *poor her*. She pops in a snowflake pill and cut to: a backyard suffocated with sunshine, contrasted only by her overly fake smile. The next vignette is just as trite. A man lies in bed with his eyes wide open. Flustered, he pops a snowflake pill, and closes his eyes, smiling peacefully. The logo dissolves and a tagline is revealed:

*Snowflakes—release your worries on your path to serenity.*

That's the world we live in, the world of the miscellaneous pill. Got a headache? Depressed? Can't sleep? Pop a pill! It will do wonders. It makes me want to vomit—but I don't actually vomit. The smell would stay in my apartment for days. It's small, but it works for me. My mother thinks it's a shit-hole, but who cares what she thinks…

Most of the sheep out there take it—the snowflake, but just because they're told to. I've never had to. Then again, I'm one of the few that can actually sleep with their eyes closed. Since the incident, I mean. It happened years ago, before I was even born, back when Bill was probably a teenager. One day, for no apparent reason—one of these random events, you could say—every single human being on this planet collapsed on the spot. You could've been driving, eating, taking a shower—it didn't matter, everyone hit the floor like a rag doll at the same exact moment and stayed there for about five solid hours, as if a sudden narcolepsy epidemic had taken over. More concerned with the "why", no one noticed the effects of the event until later that night. In addition, no one seemed to want to talk about it. They felt it was a "hush-hush" matter that was better left untouched since it couldn't be explained.

After the incident, no one was able to fall asleep with his or her eyes closed. Sleeping became an unsettling sight for whoever was awake. The sleeper suddenly became something resembling a mannequin that never blinked. But that wasn't the only pitiful aftermath, which also involved sleeping. Human beings all over the world had inexplicably lost the ability to dream.

I rub my eyes with both hands. "Haven't been able to get decent shut-eye in a week."

"Legend says when you can't sleep at night, it's because you're awake in someone else's dream," says Bill followed by a light-hearted scoff. "Yet I don't think that's the case."

*Dreams. Dreaming. The myth. The fantasy.*

"Look what I got," I say as I open my mini fridge and remove a soda can. A *secret* soda can, with an equally secret lid, manufactured to hide your favorite secret stash. The small, royal-blue bottle fits perfectly. The simple, white label reads *R³*.

# R³

His eyes widen. "Where did you get it?" he asks. "John?"

I shrug. I really can't remember.

"Have you dreamt before?"

"No. Maybe,"·I reply playing with the dreamy bottle.

"You don't remember?" asks Bill, squinting his tiny eyes, making them somehow even smaller.

"Don't you ever get that feeling where you can't tell if something is a memory or if it's something you dreamed?"

"So you dreamt?"

I shrug again. "Perhaps. But I've always slept with my eyes closed. No snowflakes for me."

My front door bangs loudly, promising to burst off its hinges. "Hammond! I know you're in there!" the voice outside shrieks. "Where's my rent you little fuck?! HAMMOND!!" The banging continues for another few seconds until the ape gives up and walks away, dragging his feet like it's his business. This happens almost every day.

I bounce the blue bottle from hand to hand. I love the swishing sound its contents make when swirled inside the glass.

"You should put all this stuff away," Bill says motioning towards the pharmaceuticals. "You don't want that kind of trouble. They'll put you away for carrying these."

I'm too distracted with the blue bottle. It's a true beauty. "Why did they make these?"

14

# R³

"What is dreaming but a desire to change reality? To make the world better? Without dreaming you become helpless to your reality. Which is why the snowflake was developed after the incident. With it, you sleep a dream-less sleep. The engorged void. It numbs down your brain. You know how no two snowflakes look alike?" Bill places a handful of beautiful 'snowflake' pills on the table. "All of these look exactly the same. In the end, we are all born to *."

*What did he say?*

"Then why did they recall it?" I ask.

"They didn't. The well ran dry." Bill jerks his head towards the blue bottle. "Where did you get it?"

"Will it make me dream?"

"It's a prepackaged dream based on recycled memories. The same dream over and over. They used to sell them when you were a kid."

I can't wait any longer. I open the bottle and gulp down its contents instantly.

"No expiration date?" he asks.

I scan the bottom of the bottle. It's scratched out. A bit too late anyway.

"How did you know where to find it?"

I shrug. Again.

I really don't.

## *Her name is Nina, she says.*

Lights pulsate.

I bounce up and down, covered in sweat. Or at least what I think is sweat. My sweat? I hold a water bottle in my hand. I look down, there's no water bottle. It happens.

The wall feels good against my back, supporting my dead weight, as my eyes get lost in the waving sea of neon.

# R³

Everyone convulses to the beat, merging into a giant blob, a creature with a single heartbeat. This makes me smile, I don't know why. My eyes slowly drift inward. I can hear my own heart pounding. More so, I can feel it has relocated—it's not buried deep in my chest, but wrapped around my head, one half on each ear.

Tiny specks of light flicker over my closed eyelids. The specks are fluid, cell-like, floating around other smaller and larger microorganisms—must be the R³. There's one main cell; it pulsates to the beat. Something suddenly perforates the membrane, quickly intertwining with the cell's contents. Invasive. Intruding. Raping.

My eyes snap open.

A girl with red hair stands in the middle of the bouncing crowd, so still. *Why isn't she bouncing?* Her eyes glimmer under the strobe lights, so much beauty, slender and supple, immaculate angelic, unearthly grace. The pounding in my chest suddenly grows louder, awoken, alive. She smiles a smile I've seen somewhere before, but for the life of me I can't figure out where or on whom. Who is she? She walks away. Away from me. I have to see her. I can't let her go. I don't know why.

I follow her striking hair. Through the crowd.

Outside the club. Large plasma screens selling me everything and anything.

# R³

Down a dark alley. Bricks holding secrets that will forever remain mysteries.

Into the darkness. Devouring everyone and anyone with no filter.

We are covered in purple and green. The neon lights from the convenience store next door bleed in through the blinds on my bedroom window. The girl wraps around me, or under me, or next to me, not sure where's up and where's down—she becomes an extension of myself.

Her name is Nina, she says. I get lost in her eyes—so many different colors and shapes, constantly moving and shifting like tectonic plates. Her kaleidoscope eyes reel me into unknown territory, like a great whirlpool of fate sucking me in.

My entire body vibrates. A strange electric current grips my muscles as she kisses my neck gently. Electrons spark whenever our skins touch. There is no pain; only pleasure. Skin on skin contact is purely orgasmic. Life flows out of me, into her, and back. *I feel so high, so... alive.*

"You know what you have to do," she says into my ear.

I nod, not knowing what she's talking about. Suddenly my entire body contracts, jerking my jaw open as a violent gasp scrapes out of my dry throat.

# R³

Sweat pours profusely from every pore as my eyes are forced wide open, and all I see is her; Nina, glowing on top of me as everything around us slowly disappears into pure, bright white. Nina.

Nina.

Nina.

Nina.

We travel. Somewhere.

We lie on a meadow amidst the tall grass. I feel like I've been there before although I have no recollection of my surroundings. The warmth feels good on my skin, sun-kissed with a golden tint. It brings out pleasant memories – memories of what? I'm not sure. I get lost in Nina's eyes once again. The gentle breeze plays with her fiery hair.

"I've met you before."

She smiles. "You saved me."

*From what?* I really can't remember.

Then the world pushes me away, as if I were falling down a deep, deep well. Nina's face grows smaller and smaller, becoming but a dim light at the end of the tunnel. It all happens so fast, before I know it I'm pushing out of the well, back into the world, except our bodies have switched. Inside Nina's body, through her kaleidoscopic eyes, I am staring at my gaunt self. Short, buzzed hair just because it's low-maintenance. Old faded shirt. There is nothing

unsettling about staring at my own face, except the familiarity of it seems to be alien. I know it is me laying across from myself, yet my eyes seem distant and estranged.

"I've met you before," my other self says to me.

As quick as it started, I sink back into the well and back out, and find myself staring into Nina's color-shifting eyes. Tears stream down her cheeks and I tell her: "We are all born to ***."

*What did I say?*

Laughter.

I'm giggling and spinning endlessly. Am I flying? I hear my mother's laughter. She holds my arms as we both spin and spin and spin, flying thanks to the grip of her hands. One slip and I could go tumbling down the hill and crack my neck. Her short, red, curly hair bounces as we fly. It's a dream-like moment. I think it's a memory but is it really real? I can't be a day over five.

The sun flares behind her, causing me to close my eyes momentarily. Her laughter changes. It's not as deep. It's more melodic. The fiery red hair tousles wildly around Nina's face as she keeps on spinning with me. Both flying endlessly. Nina and I.

"My sweet, sweet John…"

Such joy.

Had I ever known such joy?

# R³

The pink liquid pours out of the blue bottle onto a spoon—*R³*. My mother moves it around playfully, mimicking a plane; all the while I sit on my high, baby chair. Her elongated eye shadow resembles that of an Egyptian queen.

"Open wide! Open up, sweet bug. It's time to dream!"

I do.

My mother, Rose Hammond, has just turned 60. She spins joyously on the spot in the middle of an intersection. Her eyes closed, as a huge smile adorns her face. The wind pesters her old, frazzled, red hair and colorful mumu, as her spinning cycle goes on and on.

Somewhere else. A different dream.

The beautiful, elongated, metallic object cuts through the colorful, space-like, geometric environment. Lights pulse.

Lights pulse.

Lights pulse.

## I SHOULD'VE BROUGHT SOMETHING TO READ

The lack of windows and the fact that he's been inside at least three different elevators, all going down for what seemed an eternity, makes the young man with rosy cheeks think he has to be close enough to the center of the Earth to feel it's core warmth, or way past it, border lining the crust at the opposite end of the globe. Before him, the hallway stretches, long and narrow.

# R³

He wishes he'd counted his every step, but it is too late to start now. Maybe on the way back, if that is even an option. At the moment, he can only stare at the back of the two men that lead the way. One is particularly clean-shaven, obsessively immaculate. Perhaps he's just gotten a haircut, the young man thinks. The other is shorter and pudgier, and smells like Brussels sprouts—wiry black hair crawls all the way down his fat neck.

The young man with the rosy cheeks checks his wristwatch, as he follows behind silently, no questions asked. It is early morning, yet it feels like past midnight.

Never has he been so far down into the belly of the corporation. Most of the basic working-bee laboring is done upstairs—upstairs meaning ground level and above—where most of the labs and product testing facilities are; but not below the ground. Everyone knows below the ground means RESTRICTED and CLASSIFIED. Aside from it being general knowledge, there have been at least forty warning signs since starting his eternal descent.

Company has been weeding off through every rank, but even with a shortened staff, there's no reason why a simple lab technician would have enough pizzazz or clout to breathe that same processed and filtered air as the sworn-under-secrecy-scientists, without facing an immediate governmental death sentence. He certainly doesn't know why he's there, but death seems less of an option with every increasing step. *Maybe I'm getting*

# R³

*promoted?* The young man with rosy cheeks thinks. *Very improbable*, he realizes right away. In the end, he is a nobody; just one more working ant in a very large ant farm. They walk past a faded calendar showcasing cats with hats. The date shows it to be about twenty years prior to the Year Of The Now. The man with rosy cheeks has no idea what the future will bring.

After several left turns and right turns in this white maze, they finally arrive to a single, metallic looking door. The smelly, pudgy man retrieves a silvery card and swipes it across a sensor with his sausage fingers. The heavy door slides open with a high-pitched *hiss*.

Their footsteps echo on the icy tiles as they fade into obscurity. It's impossible to get an idea of the room's dimensions, as the darkness seems to extend to infinity. Judging by their in sync echoing footsteps, it is certainly quite large. Temperature drops at least thirty degrees upon entry. Their breath hangs in mid air, undisturbed.

At the center—or what can be assumed to be the center, about twenty feet away from the only door—rests a massive sphere, approximately fifteen feet in diameter. Elephantine tubes protrude from its base, like a mutant octopus, or a creature that has planted deep roots into the machinery. There is a singular door on its rough metallic surface.

# R³

Whatever it is, it's being very carefully contained, perhaps too carefully. A single symbol resembling a hieroglyph crowns the entrance: Pi, the mathematical constant.

Converted into bitmap, somewhere in that infinite string of digits is a pixel-perfect representation of both the first thing you saw on this planet, and the last thing you'll witness before your last exhale. All moments, cardinal and routine, will occur between those two points. All contained in the ratio of a circumference and a diameter. Even the young man knows that.

*What are they keeping inside?* he thinks.

He's asked to sit on a chair and keep his eyes glued on a monitor.

He's given a stopwatch, a clipboard, and a walkie-talkie device.

"Call us if anything changes," says the fat one pointing at the LCD screen. "Lunch will be brought to you. Your shift will end in four hours. Only then can you use the restroom. You must not, under any circumstance, leave this room. Do I make myself clear?"

The young man with rosy cheeks nods.

# R³

Without anything else to add, both men in lab coats turn on their heels and click-clack their way out of the cavernous room, the white door hissing behind them. Suddenly alone, the young man feels the abrupt density of silence crush his soul into smithereens.

Anxiety takes over. He looks around; the sphere looms in front of him.

*I should have brought something to read*, he thinks. Curious, he leaves the safety of his chair, and peers into the round window on the sphere's only door. Frost obstructs his vision. The interior is white – very white. In fact, the outside is mostly illuminated by the stream of whiteness that escapes through the small window, cutting through the devouring darkness like a blade.

This is now his new home, at least for the next four hours. He drops back onto the chair, taking in the enormity of his uncharted surroundings. Whatever is in there, it's not only hidden, but also secured miles deep into the earth. *And now I'm sitting next to it*, he thinks.

*I should've brought something to read.*

## *How does one grasp such nonsensical reality?*

A sledgehammer keeps banging into my skull repeatedly. Again and again. But it isn't a sledgehammer. It's my front door. I wrap both my hands around my head as I spring up, the bed sheets tangling around my leg. The pain only seems to intensify. The throbbing has a life of its own, as if a grand piano had just been dropped on my head. This is unlike any hangover I have ever felt. Not even close to the combination of all of them, all at once.

My bed is empty. Nina isn't there.

I take a step forward but instantly gravitate back onto the mattress. The entire world seems to tilt around me, like a ship being tossed back and forth, caught in a storm deep at sea. The banging continues.

I try again, one cautious step at a time, holding onto the wall, hoping it doesn't slide off leaving me off balance. The living room is a mess. That's normal. Chaos is normal. The banging on my door is normal.

It rattles. I wonder if one day it will truly burst out of its hinges.

Not today. I walk back into the bedroom closing the door behind me. I can't deal with this today. Maybe another day, maybe not, but not today, of all days. Not with tectonic plates orchestrating earthquakes in my brain.

*Not-too-dey.*

As I sink back into my old cot excuse for a bed, the banging stops. *Thank fucking god.* The lids over my eyes sink shut slowly. Peace… When the faint sound of jingling keys cut through the momentary silence.

*Oh no. Oh no. Oh no.*

My feet yank me off the cot instantly. I crawl across the wall, racing towards the front door as my apartment gets tossed back and forth by invisible waves. I'm not even ten feet away when the front door swings open.

# R³

*Oh no…*

I push myself against the wall, hoping it somehow absorbs me, encasing me with protection. But it doesn't. Fuck you, wall.

In come the dirty old military boots, the corduroy pants, the faded Hawaiian shirt, the bony elongated fingers securing the set of jingly keys back onto the worn out leather belt. His beady, psychopathic eyes, hiding behind his stringy hair, scan through the room.

Isaac is unlike any other building manager. I've never particularly gotten along with any, but he is far beyond the "getting-along" point. The way he looks at me with those possum-like eyes, always hunting, sniffing, waiting for the day he slits my throat and eats my flesh raw, licking down the bones. This may be that day. His eyes lock on my pitiful self.

"You fucking shit!" His crippling figure towers over me, as my body holds onto the wall for dear life, afraid to fall off. "Want to get evicted? Is that what you want?"

"I have your money, Isaac."

"Shit you do. Where?"

"Just—stop yelling. Calm down."

"Wassa-matter-wit-chu?" He's missing his front bottom teeth, which makes hissing rather unavoidable. "Are you drunk?"

"Just—hold on. I have to go get it…"

# R³

"Get it? From where? No more bullshit, Hammond! I'm tired of bullshit. Of shit. Of all your shit. I'll have your ass on the street by morning."

"Just—" I slowly turn, crawling my way back into the bedroom, kissing the wall, thanking it for still being there.

I dig through a few half-empty drawers. A few socks, shirts and rubber bands here and there. I find a wallet: empty. Piggy bank: empty. Glass jar: a few quarters. There's a dollar in my back pocket.

*Shit.*

I let the wall guide me back into the living room, but it soon stops, telling me something is wrong. And the wall is right.

Isaac is frozen, his back turned and his eyes glued to the coffee table in the middle of the room. The R³ bottle, the pharmaceutical bottles, an old syringe—a buffet of drugs spread all over like butter on toast.

It's over.

From behind, Isaac slowly reaches towards his waistcoat: *a gun?* He has a gun. Cold sweat trickles down my neck and down my spine. It has to be a gun. My eyes dart around the room, looking for something...

There's no time. Isaac turns briskly with his hand wrapped around a black object, but the hammer finds its way into my shaky hand before he fully faces me. Lovingly

# R³

hugged between my fingers, the hammer swings hastily, cutting through the air, finally landing on Isaac's fragile skull.

Crack.

The hammer slips out of my hand and lands on the floor with a soft thud. The object on Isaac's hand—a phone—slips out of his fingers.

"You're fucked, Hammond. Fu-fff—." Confusion spreads all over Isaac's face as blood gushes out from the side of his head. He collapses on his knees and then drops on his side. He doesn't move.

Isaac's phone emits a faint dial tone, followed by a click. "911—how may I direct your call?"

I look around in a panic, not knowing what to do. I snatch the phone and hang up. As if hoping Isaac would suddenly spring back to life, I watch him closely. But he doesn't.

I can feel my blood slowly traveling away from every capillary in my face. The cold sweat takes over. *What have I done?*

*Riiing-riiiing!!* The phone erupts. Isaac's phone? No, my phone. Somewhere. Where is it? Digging under cushions and blankets, which I doubt are mine, I find my phone. Propelled by an inexplicable force, I answer it.

*Shit.*

# R³

It's a female voice, a desperate voice. Nina's voice.

"John, do not open the door. You hear me? Do not open the door." She hangs up before I can put two words together in an attempt to unravel the unsound nature of my current situation.

Footsteps echo up the stairs. Panicking, I instinctively follow Nina's advice—*why do I trust her?*—and bolt the door shut. I press my ear against it. The footsteps fade away, traveling down the hallway. I let out a relieved sigh as blood pools around Isaac's coconut head.

Suddenly two soft knocks freeze every vein in my body. The hairs on my neck slowly rise. I lean on the door and feel the vibrations through the wood. Two more knocks. I hold my breath as the blood on the floor spreads, wrapping around my feet, inching toward the door, seconds away from seeping under.

The stranger's cell phone erupts outside. It's an unusual jingle, but there's an eerie familiarity to it. I've heard it before. The stranger doesn't pick up, but walks away. The jingle fades out with every step until I can no longer hear it. I press my ear against the door. Silence. I check on the pooling blood, but I have to look twice. There must be something wrong. There must be some kind of error, some kind of mistake. How does one grasp such nonsensical reality?

I knock a few chairs out of the way, clearing as much room as possible, exposing every little nook to the light.

# R³

But it's no use. It's time to accept the facts. Like the incident, it's time to accept the unquestionable. The blood is gone. And so is the body.

Vanished.

All of it. Gone, leaving no trace behind. Confusion trickles through my skull, clouding my brain. The pounding intensifies, only worsening as I smack my head in an attempt to reawaken. But it's pointless. No matter how many times I slap, or repeatedly close and open my eyes, the new reality doesn't change. *Where's the reset button?*

I'm left with nothing.

No blood. No hammer. No Isaac.

Nothing.

If there's anything more terrifying than dealing with a bloody problem, it's the thought of dealing with nothingness and the void it entails.

And at this exact moment, the nothingness is staring me right in the face.

## *Russian Dolls.*

My eyes are red with irritation from the water splashing, but I can't stop. Not now, not until I wake up. Splash more water. Wake the hell up. The reflection on the mirror looks hazy. Not sure if it's my face or the dirty mirror.

Since weak splashes aren't cutting it, I jump into the shower and let the water douse me entirely, realizing seconds later I'm still fully dressed.

# R³

Slapping myself doesn't seem to do much either, but the fact that I'm shivering gives me some sort of relief – at least I'm still alive. On second thought, that may not be much of a relief, considering.

"Wake up! Wake up! Wake up!"

*Wake up!* Nina's voice. Somewhere.

Oxygen fills my lungs violently as I sit up, gasping for air. It burns. I look around; everything seems to be where I left it. The buffet of drugs... the empty R³ bottle. No blood. No Isaac.

My eyes scan the living room, but my ears have some trouble adjusting. Everything sounds muffled and decibels lower, as if I were underwater. My lips are parched. There's a half-empty water bottle buried under me on the couch. I chug it instantly. Gradually my ears recalibrate and soon enough the white noise lifts like a translucent veil, leaving nothing else but the ringing phone.

It rings over and over again.

How long has it been ringing for? Was it ringing while I slept?

"Hello?" That one word hurts on its way out.

"John! Where have you been, my man?" Bill's overly-optimistic tone brings a sense of relief to my present situation. Maybe all *is* back to normal.

"I've been here."

# R³

"Been calling you for three days straight. Thought you died on me, man."

Maybe I was. "What time is it?"

"Noon. Head over. I have some new, fun stuff for you. I wanna hear about your trip."

I promise to stop by.

Like the rising tide, a sudden impulse takes over, wanting to balance out the chaos. Seeking some sense of control, even if it were a placebo in the long run, I quickly stuff a trash bag with Bill's pills, bottles, and vials. I don't need them. At least not tonight. There is no need to have them sitting out on full display. He was right, it isn't wise. Perhaps my bloody dream would materialize.

It only takes a few minutes to clean up the living room. It's still a mess, but a drug-less mess. I check my pockets for petty cash and find one dollar. Same pocket as in my dream. Coincidence? Sure, but things are never that easy.

As I open my apartment door, I find myself face to face with two officers. Two officers with boring faces, displaying their boring badges, blocking my way. I interrupted them mid-knock by the looks of it.

The fat one sputters out, "John Hammond?"

I don't speak. Not sure why.

He reads off a notepad, "John Hammond, correct?"

Suddenly their faces fold into themselves and go blank. No eyes, no mouths, no noses—just smooth skin. I fall into the well again… and fly out of my apartment, in-between the officers' heads, extending not into an apartment complex, but into what seems to be a large, nondescript space that extends to some sort of infinity. I see my door in the distance.

I fly away and everything grows smaller in size, until eventually all I can see is a speck of white against vast pools of darkness.

I realize it's only a light reflecting off the fat officer's left eye. For some reason I feel pale. I know I'm pale. I wonder if they can see it? They exchange glances. Do they see I'm pale?

"Mr. Hammond, are you alright?" the tall one butts in.

"Yes, fine."

"We wanted to ask you a few questions –"

"Regarding?"

"Your building manager has gone missing. He's been missing for three days. Have you seen him?"

*Maybe I killed him.* "No."

"Do you remember the last time you saw him?"

*Bleeding profusely on my floor a few minutes ago.* "No".

They exchange glances again. Why do they do that? "Will you please contact us if you do?"

I nod and stuff his business card in my back pocket without even looking at it. I lock my door and push through them with my large bag of drugs. They don't move an inch. *Dicks.*

# R³

"Need a hand?" the fat one scoffs.

*Dicks.*

"Why don't you stay for dinner?" my mom asks, just like she asked the time before and the time before that. No matter what I say, it never gets through, never goes into her head. Her thick skull is impenetrable; everything bounces off like ping-pong balls to the rhythm of the grandfather clock in the living room. *Tic-Toc. Ping-Pong. Tic-Pong.* Like her stuffy, overcrowded and yellowish house, this never changes. Why does she insist on living in a house with three bedrooms all by herself? Beats me. Maybe she puts her little porcelain figurines to bed. It's not like they have enough room on the shelf.

She squints, pushing her glasses back and forth like a magnifying glass, trying to read the instructions on an *InstaMeal* box. She's made them everyday for the past twenty or so years. They are the same instructions. Not sure why she feels the need to read them every single time. Frustrated, she wipes her hands on her floral mumu and pops in a snowflake pill.

"Can't ma. Busy. I've got things to do, you know?" I say as my eyes scan for small, valuable objects, knicks and knacks I could easily sell, but instead my eyes land on a large painting: *The Golden Bough* by J.M.W. Turner. I've known this painting ever since I can remember, always on the same spot, depicting some sort of dream-like, religious ceremony. To me it always looked like a day in the field, plain and simple.

Mom hollers from inside the kitchen, "Wouldn't that help your money problem?"

"Who said I had a money problem, ma?" I say as I dig through her purse, finding a lonely twenty-dollar bill. I leave it. Why bother?

"Maybe you should move in with me? That could be fun."

*Oh, Jesus.* "More like a nightmare," I mutter.

"What??"

"I'm not moving in with you, ma! I'm an independent, grown-ass man." I snap back as I play with a set of Russian Dolls, removing each of the smaller dolls and placing them in a straight line, in order of height.

She walks out of the kitchen. "Sweet bug, then how am I supposed to help you?"

For the first time today, I look at my mother. "You don't look how I remembered."

"I fixed my hair," she says fishing for a compliment.

"Can I borrow some money?"

She looks down for a second. "Are you sure you don't want to stay for dinner? I bought this new InstaMeal—"

"No, ma. God."

# R³

"Oh, alright! Here," she digs through her purse and snatches out the twenty dollars—all the cash she has. "Take it."

I don't. "Don't worry about it."

"What do you mean? Here, take it!" She shoves the cash into my back pocket and calls it a day. She wipes my face with a napkin as if I were two. I let her. Not sure why.

"I had a dream last night."

"What are you talking about? You don't dream."

"I've dreamt before. I used to tell you my dreams when I was a kid. Why are you lying?"

She digs her wrinkly fingers through my hair. "Sweet bug…"

I brush her off. I hate it when she does this. Doesn't listen.

"You're special," she adds. "The doctors feared you'd be born with a deformity. With your eyes stuck shut, or even worse, with a single eye. They wanted to terminate my pregnancy, you know? But I didn't let them." *Why is she telling me this?* "And here you are…" her eyes beam with love, "my beautiful boy."

"Ma, you're not listening. This dream –"

"You always had a vivid imagination."

"It was a dream. It was real."

She fidgets. *Why is she so nervous?* Her shaky hand digs up a card from inside her purse. She reads it and hands it over. "Take this. He's a really good doctor."

# R³

"Ma..."

"Just talk to him! He's good. He studies the brain."

He studies the brain, she says.

The brain.

Like an Algebra textbook.

It's one of those perfect autumn days in sunny California. Sunny, but cool enough to wear a hoodie. I love hoodies. There's something about the way they wrap around me, feels like a hug. Unless they're made out of a thick fabric, then it feels like I'm getting chocked or suffocated. Today is nice. Even for the Valley.

An old homeless woman has set camp at a bus stop right outside my mother's house. Her dark skin glistens in deep contrast with her hot pink jumpsuit and her golden curly hair, partially covered by a translucent neon visor. Her shopping cart is packed with plastic bottles, cans, plastic bags, and books. Every book ever printed by Pandora Publishing—makes me wonder why? Her eyes follow me everywhere—*what is she, the Mona-fucking-Lisa?*

I duck into my hoodie as I walk past her.

"Her dream has wrapped itself around your mind," she says while giving me a toothless smile. Then she bursts into sharp but broken cackles.

## R³

I hate crazy people. They scare the shit out of me.

What did she mean by that?

Her dream?

Whose dream?

**U.S. DEPARTMENT OF INTELLIGENCE**

Report: AXZU, Worldwide Blackout Incident, March 14, 21\*\*
Dated: March 20, 21\*\*
Archive Number: XYW-10390009____B
Name of the Civilian: Cassandra Walker
Age: 50
Occupation:Editor/Head of Pandora Publishing
Interviewer: Lieut. Carl Dean

**Where were you at the time of the incident?**

I was driving home, taking the same route I always do. It must have been around two in the afternoon, as I remember it being an extremely hot day. Up until then, there had been nothing out of the ordinary; traffic was as dense as expected. It was like any other day. Until it happened.

It was dark when I woke up, which sent me to an instant panic. My mind started racing. My initial thought was "what happened to the sky?" In retrospect, it almost looked as if someone had flicked an *OFF* switch. Thoughts

# R³

ranging from nuclear wars to our sun suddenly dying crossed my mind. I didn't have enough time to clearly go over each single one of them, as the next thing I noticed was the time. It was a bit over 7:00 PM. That was impossible. How had I suddenly lost five hours of time? Where had they gone? For a brief instant I thought I had a tumor, or some anomaly deceiving my brain, warping my perception. But I wasn't the only one. My neighboring cars were also completely stationary. Engines were running, but no car was moving. Drivers were stepping out of their vehicles, looking up at the dark sky in confusion. Others remained inside their cars, scared something would happen – hoping to ignore it, hoping to forget and go on with their normal lives, but this was far from normal.

The moment I arrived home, I spoke to my husband, Dr. [name deleted] who was already up to his neck attempting to put the event under a microscope. Yet he couldn't find a starting point, only a handful of hypotheses that didn't stick to anything – some to a science fiction degree – but for him everything had to be considered. As a man of not only science, but also deep-rooted metaphysics, this had become his new obsession. As you can imagine, it only worsened.

**When did you discover you had lost the ability to dream?**

Only after the fourth night. Lack of dreams usually signified deprivation of or bad sleep, at least for me. They didn't have to be linear narratives, or elaborate sequences, but after a good night's sleep, I always recalled bits and pieces. I used that as a sign of good sleep. However, no dreams came that night. Before the third night, I made it a point to check the time and go to bed early. Even drank some chamomile before going to sleep. I slept a good, solid eight hours, but couldn't recall a single dream. Not even a single image. It was as if my mind had become a vacuum for eight hours. The thought truly frightened me. Something was not right.

I wanted to be put under observation. I was worried after the event there had been some kind of damage to my brain. I immediately went to my husband, sharing my concern, when I found him sprawled on his office desk. His body was inert, his eyes wide open, unblinking. I shrieked in horror. *He's dead*, I thought. But his body suddenly reanimated, as if woken by my scream. I was terribly frightened.

Nonchalantly, even annoyed to a certain extent, he adjusted his glasses up the bridge of his nose and asked, *what's with the ruckus?*

I explained everything immediately. I trust no one else would have believed me, but he knew I wasn't the type to feed into superstition or exaggerations. We ran a few tests and concluded that, not only were we not able to dream during sleep, but we were also unable to close our eyes during. REM had suddenly become a thing of the past. This made absolutely no sense, biologically nor chemically.

# R³

**What results was Dr. [name deleted] able to extract?**

Everything was submitted to your department as requested. We really do not understand how or why this happened, but I don't believe that's the true issue at hand. I fear what will happen next. That's the big mystery, the unnerving question mark. Our existence has been changed completely, yet the change is deceivingly minimal. It's not as if we woke up missing all four limbs – we lost something untraceable, something deeply rooted in our subconscious. There's no physical evidence of such a loss. What can we do? How will we adapt? How will we change now that we live in a dreamless world? That's what's keeping me up at night.

## *All infinite possible potentials and outcomes in one.*

Not really sure whose living space is more crowded, ma's or Bill's—or why do I even surround myself with such chaos. I'm gonna say Bill's, mainly because his place is smaller. He lives in an RV—a large RV—, but an RV nonetheless. Home-on-wheels; the American style. He hates that. It's almost as if he's made it a point to personalize his home slash vehicle, to the extent of hoarding. There's paraphernalia everywhere. Crystals, candles, incense (all

# R³

burning at the same time, mind you), small gongs, big gongs, chimes, framed Hindi images, framed Jesus images, a small Buddha, the solar system, psychedelic and geometric images, beads, large seating pillows he got from India and lots and lots of neon. It's a minefield.

Bill moves swiftly among the clutter, preparing an InstaMeal in his tiny kitchen. He plops three small jell-o-like cubes into three bowls and adds a drop from a dropper to each. They instantly sizzle, as if suddenly boiling. The jell-o-like cubes immediately turn into a liquid—something resembling a noodle soup. That's the basic chemistry of it. He hands two bowls to a crystal-smoking couple sitting in a corner. The other, he brings to me. Sun is almost down.

"You had Nina's Dream," he assures, twitching his nose like a rabbit. "That's Nina's Dream. You say you met her? That woman, from your dream?"

"Last night – wait, two nights ago, before the dream. After I drank the R³."

"You met Nina?"

"Yes. Red-head? Kaleidoscope eyes? Why?"

"It's unusual. That's all."

The wheels in his brain are turning, that much I can tell, but he doesn't push any further, so neither do I.

"It's the R³, right? You've had her dream before?" I ask.

"I have. Where did you get it?"

He won't drop it. "I don't know. It slipped my mind."

"But you knew where to find it?"

"I think so. I don't know. It's almost as if I put it there myself. I just knew."

"But then it slipped your mind?"

"Slipped away." Attempting to change the subject, "I killed a man, Bill."

"What do you mean?"

"My building manager. I smashed his skull in with a hammer."

"Jesus. Did you call the police?"

"No. Well – there was a bit of a problem. He vanished." There was no other way of saying it.

Bill's eyes narrow. "Vanished? Did he walk away?"

"No, he was gone. Entirely. No blood, nothing, almost as if it had never happened. Except then, I woke up. Again. I thought I might've dreamt it, but you said Nina's Dreams were—"

"…prepackaged dreams," he interrupts, then ponders on this, biting his lower lip. "Are you awake now?"

"I'm not sure."

"It's hard to tell the difference between the sea and the sky on the horizon. Your worlds are mixing," he says. "Waking life and dream. But John, is this your dream or is it Nina's?"

"How do I know for sure?"

Bill leans in, secretively. "Do you believe in parallel dimensions? Black holes?"

# R³

"Like—aliens?" *Dumb answer.*

"There seems to be a warp in this reality. I've noticed it too," his eyes look around, searching for who knows what. "It started three days ago. Our reality is off-axis. It's been uncalibrated."

"How do you know?"

"Come with me." He leads me towards the window. Outside, the sun has set, but the sky still has a faint glow of light blue. "There. Do you see it?"

At first I don't, but I squint hard and finally see it. Amidst a small clump of clouds, a narrow, undulating patch of color streaks faintly pulsates. It almost looks like light refracting off a bubble, but on the clouds. It's small, but it's there. "What is that?"

"Not sure. Could be a hole in the stratosphere. Maybe a portal. It appeared three days ago." He goes back to his seating cushion. "This is a syncopation, interrupting the regular flow, the regular rhythm."

"How do you fix it?"

"Only the absolute can." *The what?* "Only *it* can calibrate it; neutralize it; merge all the loose and continuously multiplying time lines into one."

"Time lines?"

"All the infinite possible potentials and outcomes in one. The primordial one that contains all numbers. Infinity within the water drop. The all-seeing-eye," he says, his own eyes growing wide.

# R³

I feel my eyebrows suddenly furrowing, creating some sort of intense wrinkle on my brow, as if my brain were straining, trying hard to grasp this concept. But of course it doesn't. "You're shitting me?"

Bill shakes his head. He's dead serious.

"Where do I find this... eye?"

"You don't."

I can feel my frown growing back.

Bill continues... "I read it in a manuscript years back—in an old diary. I used to think it was a work of fiction, a goose tale, a scam for the weak of mind, you know? Or part of a vivid dream—since a dreamer wrote it years ago, but now... now I know... it's real. It's factual. It has to be."

"What is? What is this *thing*?"

"A point in space that contains all other points. Anyone who gazes into it can see everything in the universe from every angle simultaneously, without distortion, overlapping, or confusion," he says as he licks his thin lips.

That's not possible, I think. "That's impossible," I say.

"It's real, John. Just like you. Just like me." He leans in, stressing even further secrecy. "I've felt it. I was a lab researcher at the institute that developed R³. I don't know how to explain it, but I felt it, through her, through Nina. And I've been looking for it ever since. And somehow, I know you—don't ask me how, but I know—you, you are supposed to take me to it."

"Me?? How am I involved in this?"

# R³

"The universe is telling you to find it. It wants you to find it."

"Why me?"

"Why not?" He's serious. I hate it when he's serious. "Perhaps because you're the only one listening. You can dream, John. Ever since the incident, no one has been able to dream. Only empty sleep with open eyes. Millions killed themselves because of it. They quickly developed the snowflake as if to paint destruction pink, trying to give the dream-less sleeper some grace; allowing them to sleep with their eyes closed. That was until Nina. She could dream. And she could dream loud. She showed it to me. The absolute. I felt it. And then you show up, telling me you met Nina? You are taking me back to it."

"We met by chance, Bill."

"The universe happened by chance," he snaps right back. "John, you must find it. It's of utter importance."

"I need to clear my head."

This is not happening. This can't be happening. I will not be a victim of circumstance.

I place some crystals into a pipe as Bill paces back and forth, bouncing the issue around his head. He's setting off on a small, but steady, path to obsession. He looks out the window repeatedly.

I turn to the other side and lie on the floor as I inhale and exhale, trying to relax, trying to escape this madness. I stare at the only empty space in Bill's RV, the chaos-free ceiling. Untouched. Untainted. Unpolluted.

Inhale.

Exhale.

Lying on the floor.

Inhale.

Exhale.

As if suddenly dreaming with my eyes open.

## AN UNRELIABLE AUTHOR

The white stream covers him entirely, as if he were trapped at the bottom of a well and the sun was his only beam of hope.

The young man with rosy cheeks checks his stopwatch and the LCD monitor. He makes a note on his clipboard. The monitor, quite similar to a heart-monitoring device, beeps as a continuous green line blinks up and down.

# R³

The main door hisses open. The fat scientist stomps all twenty feet without saying a word. He swipes his card granting him access into the spherical mass. The smell of Brussels sprouts lingers.

The door remains open long enough for the young man with rosy cheeks to peer inside. In the middle of the room, upright, is a large white capsule, large enough to fit a full person—it resembles a smooth iron lung. An assisted breathing device inhales and exhales heavily, mechanically. The capsule is designed in such a way that its contents are not exposed. A bundle of thin IV tubes extract a glowing yellowish liquid from inside the capsule, feeding it into a slick, egg-shaped dialysis machine.

The door slides shut obstructing his view.

The young man with rosy cheeks pulls on his white lab coat in a failed attempt to keep warm. His breath materializes every time he exhales.

The door slides open letting the fat man out. It slides shut behind him. He stares down at the young man, despite being way shorter, and then proceeds to stomp his way out.

Alone again.

The young man waits a few seconds before digging into his lab coat, and retrieves a small, thin book, almost the size of a pocket-sized moleskin. He goes to the first page:

# R³

## NOTE FROM THE EDITOR

When I first came across the pages from the missing settler's diary, I couldn't really put a finger on what it truly was; a work of fiction posing as a diary? A fabrication with intensions of deception? Or an actual account, about a legitimate turn of events? After years of close examination, I concluded I had no option but to lean towards the latter. Even after verifying the accuracy of its date of origin through professional carbon testing, there was no way of proving if this person was who he said he was, nor if he saw what he said he saw. As far as my own personal investigation was able to reach, I never came across an individual by that name during that specific period, in any of the surrounding towns – which could as well have been rather spotty. The only reason I decided to believe its contents were truthful was simply because I wanted to believe. However, as an objective publisher, I managed to keep my distance, steering away from any kind of bias when putting the document together. Although at least 60% of the pages are missing [or were removed], I did my most best to follow a chronological order, based on the dates listed on each entry. For the entries that were undated, a separate chapter was included, as there was no sure way to decide if they should come before or after the dated entries. For the reader's sake, these were included at the end of the compilation, so as to serve as an epilogue. Any scratched out words or sentences (as there were many) were, either completely erased, based on the quality of possible interpretation, or were rewritten with possible word options, trying to remain as close as possible to the original wording patterns.

There's no "best way" to describe or to preface the author's experience. Whether it was a product of his imagination, a hallucination, or "real", is up to the reader to decide, but as he himself explains towards the end of his last entry, his mathematical background prevented his trained brain to reach any illogical conclusion, always resorting to more grounded calculations and logistics. Yet to this day, he has remained an unreliable author.

Cassandra Walker,
Pandora Publishing, Inc.

The man with the rosy cheeks turns the page, coming face to face with the beginning of the manuscript.

# R³

 

*I wasn't sure how long I had been walking for, but I knew I had to be over three miles away from the camp, heading north. A small stream had been keeping me company. After a few miles, I finally reached the end of the stream, or more so, its beginning; a tranquil basin, about thirty feet in diameter. I approached its gentle shore. A steep cliff directly in front of me hugged the basin between us. Trees blocked the end of the mountain, keeping it out of sight. I couldn't see or hear a waterfall or set of streams anywhere around, which meant this basin had been born from underground, and not from an ice cap above. Based on my basic geology knowledge, there should be an underwater cave not too far from the surface, leading into an underground lake, or to an even bigger basin, which, in turn, feeds the one before me with fresh water. Such a kind of lake can actually be very dangerous to swim in. The force propelled by the currents going in and out of the basin and undertow, create a whirlpool that could instantly pull you down into the depths of underground rivers, causing your almost immediate death, either by the rocky interiors, or by drowning. It's not far from the truth to say I knew better than to go swimming into such an unpredictable environment, but it was something stronger than my intellect and logic that drew me in. That is when the "object" in question revealed itself.*

*At first I thought it was only a rock, creating a deceiving reflection on the surface, but upon closer observations, it proved to be that there was no rock in that location—at least not that close to the surface, as the lake did indeed run deep.*

*My second theory was: perhaps it's some kind of light fragmentation. On the clear surface of the lake, I could distinctively see an object being reflected, an object, which technically should have been floating about ten feet over the lake; about six feet in front of me. However, there was no object hovering above the surface. In fact, there was nothing between where I was standing and the treetops.*

*I did a few rounds around the basin's circumference and was able to climb onto the cliff. It gave me an even clearer view of the lake's surface and its enigmatic reflection. Simply put, there was nothing there to reflect. And if there was, my eyes couldn't see it, but for some reason the lake could mirror it, as if it were some trickery or illusion. Yet, that's quite impossible.*

*Several hours must have passed, because I could no longer see the sun directly above me. It was hiding between dense branches. Expecting the*

# R³

*reflection to move once the sun's position had changed was unsatisfactory. In fact, the location of the invisible object, remained fixed on the lake's reflection.*

*Having disproved every possible explanation to try and describe such an anomaly, and having found none, I moved onto making an attempt at detailing the object.*

*The object could only be described as a giant bubble, constantly shifting and therefore creating its own light reflections and refractions. If it truly had been underwater, it could only have been some type of giant jellyfish, but as explained before, this object was not underwater. That was not a possibility.*

*I lost myself, drawn in by the playful ripples on the water's surface. I was filled with sudden peace and serenity. That is when I found myself falling into the lake.*

## *You are dead, right?*

The computer screen illuminates my face. It's past midnight. I love visiting the library late at night. It's so quiet. So dark. So empty. Peaceful. I do a quick search for *Nina* but get zero results. Next, I try *Nina's Dream*, but no results once again. This doesn't make sense. There should be something, there has to be something. What are my choices? I try $R^3$—can't go wrong with that, a product which had been on sale on every shelf for a few years straight.

The monitor goes instantly crazy with pixelation followed by a black screen. Then it lights up again, giving me the loading wheel. For some reason it had automatically restarted. It looks like something doesn't want to be found. Or something wants to be forgotten.

What if Bill is right? What if dreaming was suddenly seen as a disease? A sickness? And $R^3$ as a drug, a medium to achieve some sort of personal growth? What if we one day stopped breathing? I wonder if that would suddenly become forbidden as well.

My ears are chill now that it's colder. That's when the hoodie comes in. Luckily the winter wave hasn't hit yet, but it will come, just like last year, and the year before. I wonder if I'll make it to this winter. Not sure why that thought crossed my mind.

The streets are empty. You can smell the morning dew. It's funny how something as minute as smell can shift your emotions entirely, triggered by some obscure hidden memory.

I look up. No stars tonight. No moon either. However I catch a shimmering glimpse of the hole in the stratosphere. Could that really be what Bill makes it to be? It could be

# R³

anything. But one thing's for sure, it's there. And you can't ignore it. I wonder if other people can see it? As I look around, there's no one to ask—no surprise since it's about five in the morning—except for one person, about twenty feet behind. A lonely shadow lingering, trying but failing to muffle its echoing footsteps on the dirty concrete. I speed up, uneasy, try to lose it by turning around a corner.

A few seconds later I hear it behind me again. It's following me. *Someone is following me.*

I walk into my apartment and lock the door. The shadow isn't there anymore. At least I can't see him from my window. Either way, he's outside, I'm inside. It's good.

Not sure why, but I'm unable to fall asleep. My eyelids refuse to make contact with each other, so I decide to go on a scavenger hunt through my fridge. It lasts fifteen seconds. Would've been longer if I'd had any real groceries inside and not just a frozen water bottle and my secret soda can. I pull out the only other consumable item—a real soda can. I sit at the kitchen table and take a sip. For some reason my eyes refrain to open fully. My eyelids feel heavy even though I'm not tired. Rubbing my temples doesn't seem to help.

Suddenly someone walks behind me, across the room. I look up and notice the stranger immediately, yet he doesn't startle me. It's not the stranger from outside—that, I know for sure. Nonetheless, I feel like I should be panicking a bit, or at least show some faint emotion of surprise. But that's

# R³

not the case. Impressively calm, I observe the intruder closely and take another sip from my drink.

Partially hidden in shadow, he goes through my cabinets and pulls out an InstaMeal. He follows the steps carefully: places it in a bowl, adds the drops, lets it sizzle, and brings it over to the table, sitting on the opposite end. Without acknowledging me, he starts eating and slurps, loudly. His stringy hair dips into the bowl every time he leans in. It's a bit disgusting, but eating manners aside, he seems to be fine. No blood, no sign of violence. Almost as if I'd never smashed a hammer into his brittle skull. In fact, I would even go as far as saying Isaac has never looked better.

*I have to be dreaming.*

*Why does he eat so loud?*

I hadn't moved an inch, when Isaac looked up abruptly, locking deep into my eyes. Strange.

*Can he read my mind? Maybe I should stop asking so many stupid questions. Stupid, stupid, stupid.*

*Man, I'm hungry.*

An extra bowl slides out of seemingly nowhere, stopping exactly in front of me. Interesting. Isaac resumes eating his own soup. Slurp. Slurp.

*The sea and the sky on the horizon,* like Bill said. *Maybe this is all a big riddle. A puzzle. A riddle that will either unlock the secrets of the universe, or one that will drive me mad, like the crazy prophetic hobo outside my mother's house.*

Isaac keeps eating. I can't seem to lift the spoon, so I stare at it blankly. Too many questions floating inside my head to worry about food, no matter how hard my stomach is churning.

*I'm having dinner with a dead person. You are dead, right?*

I'm sure Isaac heard me, but decided to ignore my question. Instead, he stopped eating, stretched his fingers and—one hand at a time—grabbed onto the air and pulled, as if he had just caught a fly. I see no other way to describe it. Except the air refracted as soon as he did, exposing color streaks similar to the hole in the stratosphere. Once both his hands pulled these refracting, now geometric, color streaks, and brought them to the center, they instantly gave shape to a solid, *real*, object. In this case: a soda can. A soda can made out of thin air.

Fizz. Isaac opens it and takes a large gulp, "aaaah…!" He exposes his Cheshire cat smile, as his body slowly evaporates leaving only his crooked grin behind.

*Hmm…*

# *There's a syncopation in reality.*

My mother rarely has the best of ideas, but I'll admit, this head doctor sparked my interest. It probably wouldn't have at any other given point, but based on my current situation and my late snack with a dead man, I figured *why not*?

A white clock ticked on the wall loudly. White fluorescent lights reflected off the white tiles, creating a surreal dream-like environment, closely resembling the Baroque room from *2001: Space Odyssey*. If you don't know what I'm talking about and haven't seen the movie, perhaps you should. In all seriousness, get your fat ass up and watch it.

The main difference between both rooms was that this one had an obvious way out. An exit. I could see it; same door I came in through. Yet I couldn't get up, I couldn't seem to leave. Maybe it's just an illusion—me leaving. Maybe the door doesn't exist anymore and all that's left is a memory of a threshold I went through. Maybe. But it's still a door, whether it's an exit or not. A door. I guess the other room didn't have a door. At least a proper door. Perhaps I'm better off with no way out.

"John Hammond?"

That's my name. The man's voice, in par with his suede turtleneck and slick hair, is both clean and flawless. Tiny wrinkles crown the outside of his eyes hidden under spotless, black-framed glasses, fitting like the perfect jigsaw piece on his mature, yet young, thirty-year-old-something face. The impeccably manicured hands, the symmetrical tie, the glistening, gold watch and the black Prada shoes, so polished I almost got lost in my own reflection.

"John Hammond?" he repeats, looking down at his clipboard, as if to double check since I'm the only lost soul currently in the limbo room.

# R³

"Welcome. Please step inside," he says with an all-pearly-white-smile as I make way into his office. A polished bronze plaque neatly adorns his door, boldly displaying his name: *Dr. John Hammond, Ph.D.*

I know. The name. One of those funny things, I tell you.

*Funny.*


The Baroque patterns spread into the molding of his office. I let my body sink into the leather Chaise Lounge. How cliché. It has that distinctive new smell. Makes you wonder how many folks laid here appreciating their playful senses, and how many others were too busy yapping their problems away to notice.

"Are you nervous?" he asks, maybe because I'm fidgeting. I'm not really sure why I'm fidgeting.

"Should I be?"

"There's no reason to be nervous. Though it's an understandable fear."

"Fear of what?"

"Fear of being crazy. Fear of being shunned by society."

"Don't all mental patients insist they're perfectly fine and it's the world around them that's crazy?" I snap back.

"John, I'm not a crazy doctor. Everyone has issues. Those who you'd call *normal* people do too. Sometimes that's all it takes to help someone; to listen. And that's what

I do. I listen. There's no voodoo to it." He flashes those pearly whites again. "How can I help you?"

"Can I be honest?"

"Please."

"I think this is bullshit," *yes, that's my opening statement,* "pretending to get into someone's head, fixing their brain, their problems, when all you do is sit there and take their money. Some people don't want to be helped. Depressed people enjoy being depressed. You enable them. You're their drug."

"Is that so?"

"Like some vicious cycle. Making the same mistakes over and over, no matter how many times you tell them not to."

"Do you often see the world through other people's eyes, John?"

"No."

"Why don't you let me try and help you? You're here, in my office. You don't have to come back if you don't want to, but we can at least use this allotted time, so as to not waste your trip." *Ha, trip.* "What brought you here, today?"

I can't help but roll my eyes, while having to admit the man is right. It was my decision to walk into his office. It was my decision to lie on this delicious smelling couch. It was all my decision. So I could either stare at the ceiling for

# R³

the next hour or at least play ball. *My* decision. But is it really?

"I had a dream." I begin. I know of no other place where to begin.

"In your sleep?"

"Yes, in *my* sleep, when else do people dream?"

"As you know, John, people don't really dream anymore."

"Well, this is not about people, this is about *me*. Me, me, me, me," I shrill like a Chihuahua, "I've been able to dream since I can remember, but only in rare spurts. I used to dream a lot when I was a kid but everything went dark after that. Until a few nights ago. I feel like I'm losing control."

"Are you afraid of losing control?" he writes down whatever it is shrinks write down during sessions.

"We'll that's a stupid question."

"Nothing you say is stupid—" typical condescending shrink answer.

"I feel like I'm entering a new reality. Yet part of me remains in the old one. I feel—torn."

"There's always only one reality, John. A physical object, as you are, can only be in one place at one time. Einstein proved that. Is that what's troubling you?"

"There's a syncopation in reality."

# R³

"Even the most extravagant of syncopations are still part of music. They are not an error, but part of the overall flow and rhythm. Tell me about your dream."

"Pleasant memories, I guess."

"Your memories?"

"No. They were Nina's. I think."

That's when he stops writing. I can feel his pen touching the yellow notepad. I can feel the friction. But it is static.

After a brief pause, he continues. "You drank R³?" His demeanor has changed. As if a switch inside his brain had suddenly flicked on instantly giving me his full attention.

"Yes. But I didn't have Nina's prepackaged dream. I was in it, in her dream. We were sharing it. I looked it up but couldn't find anything on the subject. As if it had been erased completely. Every record."

He twiddles with his pen. "How is this dream affecting you?"

"I had this weird feeling—as if I had met her before. No—I know, I've met her before."

"Before the dream?"

"Yes." I say yes.

"Dreams are fabrications, collages of memories. You may have seen her face somewhere, but in fact, this woman your mind created, does not exist. At least not as you think she does. She's not real John, only a fabrication of a wild, unnaturally induced dream."

# R³

"No. I met her a long time ago. And I saw her again that same night, before the dream."

"You saw her? In waking-life?"

"That's not everything. I was *her* for a short moment. Almost as if we had switched bodies and I was suddenly seeing the world through her eyes, not mine. Feeling what she was feeling. Her pain."

"That's not possible," his tone changed. He felt... angry.

"Why?"

He didn't have enough time to reply. He probably didn't want to either. His cell phone erupted, splicing our conversation in half instantly. I looked down, embarrassed, not sure why. Until I realized I had heard that jingle before. It was the same, broken melody I had heard outside my apartment that morning Isaac bled to death between my feet. Why does he have the same jingle? And why do I feel like I've heard it before? Before now. Before Isaac. Before before.

"Is this melody upsetting you?" He's been staring at me closely, studying my face, my every move. "My apologies, I usually keep it off during sessions."

A sudden invisible wall seems to grow around me as I fidget again, looking away, avoiding eye contact. I'd like to crawl back into my apartment now.

"It sounds like the beverage had an unexpected chemical reaction with your body and has started acting as a hallucinogen would," he begins his so-called diagnosis. "Most hallucinogenic states can have self-consistent histories and rules. They can also include time effects making it seem like time goes on indefinitely, or to have been going indefinitely. Which also happens when you sleep. A twenty minute nap can feel like a full-night's sleep."

I'll admit that seems to explain a lot, everything in fact, but it doesn't fit. It's too perfect. It's not right.

"What if this reality is an extended continual dream and death is when you wake up?" I ask.

He stares at me blankly.

"A dream is a reality when you're in it, right?" I add. "Reality is a dream, and then memories are what's left when you are out of it."

"Then John, the solution is quite simple," he begins. "You need to open your eyes – and wake up."

*Wake up.*

That simple.

*Reuse. Redream. Recycle.*

The same image of my mother appears before my eyes, as she attempts to feed me R³ by the spoonful, cackling like a hen with her Egyptian queen eye shadow.

"Open wide! Time to dream."

The TV is clearly on as its white light flickers against the intricate wallpaper, switching from levels of high to low intensity, but due to its current angle, the screen remains unseen. Whatever dialogue or music was playing then was not registered in the imprint of my memory.

"There you go, sweet bug!" she says as she reveals her crooked smile. "Now let's get some for mommy!"

Following her very carefully orchestrated eight o'clock routine, she pours herself some of the pink liquid before quickly chasing it with a big gulp of red wine, until there's not but a drop left. The process doesn't quite end there. She refills her glass laughing joyously, overpowering whatever soundtrack plays on the disregarded TV box.

It's not until the hyena wail ends that I can clearly hear what plays on the box. It's the haunting jingle. The same one Dr. Hammond seemed to have selected, out of all the infinite options, for his phone. I instantly bop my tiny body off my favorite couch towards the TV. I come face to face with it, as if preparing for a Spaghetti Western duel.

*This is it.*

*The moment of truth.*

*What are you?*

On that beautifully shaped rectangle, perfectly framed in the center, Nina's face materializes out of white, leading into the beginning of a commercial. Her skin radiates, comparable only to how one would imagine an angel. Her striking hair immaculately tied back into a perfect bun. Her perfect smile. Her movements enigmatic and minimal, giving her presence a surrealistic quality—she was perfectly robotic.

Her full lips part on cue.

"Reuse. Redream. Recycle. Making all of your dreams come true."

As her flesh dissolves into whiter than white, the glistening blue bottle takes her place with a caption under it:

**R³**

**Making Your Dreams A Reality**

I press my tiny, four-year-old hands against the screen, taken aback by how easily they blend in, dissolving into her magnetic whiteness, mixing in with the electric static, becoming one.

I find it incredibly bizarro how much Dr. Hammond's home resembles his private office. And this is not a mere matter of sterile taste and lack of a warm color palette, but to the extent of impersonal décor. The single college diploma, framed in what could best be described as expensive, glossy wood, surrounds itself by a collection of thick books, taking over your usual family vacation picture spots on the shelf.

# R³

No Christmas postcards; nothing. Almost as if no memories had been stored in this environment, or non that wanted to be openly displayed.

*How did I get here? Why am I here? Is this a dream?*

A medium sized crate holds another mound of books on his round glass table. A few swim around the crate like satellites or moons orbiting a large planet. I grab the one on top: *THE GOLDEN BOUGH: A STUDY IN MAGIC AND RELIGION* by Sir James George Frazer. Another one reads *THE MONADOLOGY* by G. W. Leibniz. I flip through it carelessly – chunky text. Until the pages abruptly come to a halt:

> *Now, as in the Ideas of God there is*
> *an infinite number of possible*
> *universes, and as only one of them*
> *can be actual, there must be a*
> *sufficient reason for the choice of*
> *God, which leads Him to decide upon*
> *one rather than another.*

Stuck in the middle of the book, both clumsily hidden and incredibly inconspicuous, sits a small brown manuscript with a large black symbol on the cover.

For no particular reason, I look up and find myself facing a stainless steel-encased oval mirror. Everything seems to be in order, except for the fact that my face is not there. In a similar fashion to my encounter with the officers outside my apartment, my face suddenly lacks eyes, nose, a mouth… leaving nothing behind but a smooth, blank canvas of skin.

Somewhere else…

…In a different dream…

…In the vacuum, where muted sounds resembling crackles erupt at no specific interim…

The beautiful, elongated, metallic object cuts through the colorful, space-like, geometric environment. Getting closer.

And closer.

And closer.

Closer.

## *I died, but then I was reborn.*

*Where am I?*

My eyes open halfheartedly, blinking a couple of times as they adjust to the blazing ball of fire. Someone plays with my hair forcing me back to sleep as I try furiously to stay awake. I slowly get a general sense of my bearings as alertness seeps into my brain. I force myself to sit up. I look around. I was sleeping on a bench. A bus stop bench. I had been sleeping on the bus stop bench outside my mother's house where the loony homeless woman with the shopping cart sits on a daily basis. Why or how did I get here? Your guess is as good as mine. As to why she was playing with my hair, I have a few hypotheses; none of which are worth mentioning.

The top of my head itches. Great, I think, loony gave me lice. Or worse—fleas. Fleas lay eggs on your bed, your pets, your furniture. They spread. Vicious parasites. At least lice stay on your head.

Her toothless trap opens, crapping out some mumbo jumbo: "You are not a drop in the ocean. You are the entire ocean in a drop."

I stare into her unblinking eyes, glimmering with intense passion. Could this woman be speaking the truth? Perhaps. But the squawking cackle that followed instantly shattered our newfound connection.

Ma prepares an InstaMeal while I scan through the kitchen cabinets. It's supposed to be breakfast. At least that's what the diagram on the box suggests. She places the jell-o-like cube on a bowl.

I catch a glimpse of my reflection. I look like shit. The bags under my eyes are as big as plums, but I can't tell whether it's from oversleeping or lack of sleeping.

# R³

"Are you sure you don't want to take a shower? The meal needs a few minutes to cool down."

I tell her I'm good.

I pocket one of those fancy new LED lighters. Don't think she saw me, and if she did, she's doing a great job pretending otherwise.

*The great pretender.*

"Are you feeling alright?"

*Why would she say that?*

"You barely ate."

Oh. I'm sitting at the dinner table. It seems I had gotten glued to my reflection in the bowl. More like the silhouette of my reflection, since you can't really tell my features apart. I hadn't eaten anything. She was already done.

This has been a recurring thing—time passing, me not noticing.

"Not hungry," I tell her.

She pops a snowflake and chases it with a glass of water.

"You shouldn't take those."

"They make me feel good. Did you get around seeing that doctor?"

"Did he give you those?"

"He's good, isn't he?" she shoots back. It's like talking to a wall, no one listens.

"You remember R³, don't you?"

# R³

"R³? No—no. What is that?" she asks.

"A drink."

Her expression: blank.

"You used to give it to me as a kid," I add.

More blank in the abyss of blankness.

"What drink? I didn't give you a drink…"

"The dreaming drink, ma!"

She frowns, hard, straining her brain, as if digging deep down into the old chambers of her memory bank.

"Oh, yes! The drink!"

*Halle-fucking-lujah!*

"How lovely it was to dream, even if it was a prepackaged dream," she adds, reminiscing.

"The girl, in the dream, did I ever meet her?"

"No, I don't think so. No."

"Nina?"

"Sweet bug, I don't remember. I'm sorry but it's all very fuzzy."

"Maybe if you hadn't been blacked out half of the time it wouldn't be fuzzy."

She instantly looks down, forcing a meek half-smile, embarrassed. I regret saying that instantly. I'm an asshole. No need to poke the wound, no matter how much truth infected it. I try my best to change the subject.

"There's a homeless woman loitering outside. You should call the cops."

"She's here??" She instantly rises and rushes to the kitchen fetching an extra bowl. "I haven't seen her in four days!"

"Do you know her?" but she rushes out of the house, too excited to formulate an answer. "Ma!"

*Goddammit.*

The second the bowl is handed to her, Ms. Cuckoo digs her hand in, scooping out noodles like a wild animal. I observe, feeling my face go sour, unable to hide my disgust. God, she slurps so loud. Louder than Isaac.

"What are you doing?" I finally ask my mother.

"She used to be here all the time. Until she disappeared one day."

"How come I hadn't seen her before?"

"I died," Ms. Cuckoo butts in, amidst her slurps. "But then I was reborn. After three days."

My mother smiles, finding her lunacy adorable in every sense of the word. I think her brain may be as warped as this woman's.

"Ma, she's obviously a nut."

"Johnny!" she whacks my arm as if I were ten.

"I was reborn, to deliver a message," crazy says, slurp, slurp. "I have information that can save lives."

"A message you say?" my mother feeding coal to the fire.

# R³

"Stop encouraging her."

"A message. For you," says the slurping monster as she points her boney, noodle-wrapped finger at me, like the Greek prophet Cassandra, cursed with visions that would go forever ignored.

A sudden feeling of discomfort takes over my body. I feel sick to my stomach. What could this woman possibly have to say to me? Every word she mutters only adds up to incoherent sentences. What could she possibly have to tell me? What could be so important?

Maybe she knows. Maybe she knows everything. Maybe she knows what's happening to me, and how my world is starting to unravel. Maybe she can help me and show me the way out.

Maybe.

"And what's the message?" my mother leans in, naturally curious.

The woman looks up, deer in the headlights. "Message? What message?" *Slurp*.

I can feel my face turn beat red. I stomp away before I make the completely impulsive decision of smashing that woman's head into the pavement and beating her senseless with a stick.

How could I believe she could help me? Even if it was for a split-second, how did I let myself be suckered into her broken brain?

# R³

I feel so stupid. Deceived by my own brain. I want to go back to that bowl of soup, back to that dark silhouetted reflection, and allow myself to be taken by it, consumed, fed into the whirlpool towards the void.

I'm not going to let it deceive me again.

## I MUST NOT LET MY MIND DECEIVE ME

*October 15, 1591*

*I didn't drown, but I remember being underwater for hours. That of course, is not possible. The possibility of having hit my head against a rock when falling into the lake still lingers, although I haven't been able to find wound or bruise. However, that didn't stop the disorientation from overtaking me. I do remember falling,*

# R³

*splashing through the surface, having no sense of alarm or fear as my body weight sank into the infinite depths of the basin.*

*Once lucidity crept back in, my immediate reaction was to swim towards the surface, sure that I'd soon be running out of air, but I soon faced a new complication. It could've been partially due to my disorientation, but I couldn't differentiate up from down. This shouldn't have been a long-term issue as down would logically be darker and up would have the sun blazing through, guiding me out. However, this was different. Darkness was around me, but the sun beamed from both above and below. This statement obviously contradicts itself. That is, by all laws abiding physics and reality, in one word, impossible. Time wasn't a luxury I could sit on as I debated on the unnatural causes of such an anomaly, so I quickly made a choice and pushed up—if that indeed was "up"—towards one of the two beaming suns.*

*Only a few seconds went by before I knew I had made the right choice. As I kicked towards the surface, I could clearly see the enigmatic bubble materialize on the other end, refracting the sun rays like a diamond.*

# R³

*It must now be close to six o'clock as the clouds have that pink streak, common during summer evenings. I spent the last two hours sitting on the rocky shore, pondering of the above-mentioned events and losing myself in the beauty of the bubble and its light refraction game.*

**Note from editor:** the two following pages were hard to salvage. By the looks of it, the author had attempted to draw the bubble or the basin itself, but humidity or possibly even damage by his own hand, left only but a blob of charcoal-like smudges. [Pandora Publisher]

*October 17, 1591*

*I have found myself lost. After walking downstream for what must have been two miles, I stopped and set camp. On any other occasion, I would have had no problem enduring a few more miles, but this was unfamiliar territory. Even with the river by my side as my guide, I knew I had lost my bearings. I didn't recognize my surroundings and I did not want to run into a wild animal come sunset. That night, I fell asleep with ease.*

*Morning birds made sure I was awake and ready to continue my journey by sunrise. It was around noon, when I concluded I was irrevocably lost. After walking another five to seven miles, I realized I should have reached the village by now, but it was nowhere to be found—nor were there any signs of my initial track towards the basin.*

*Perhaps I would never find my village. Perhaps I, in fact, did not make the right choice when exiting the lake. Perhaps I exited somewhere else, somewhere new, somewhere where giant bubbles levitate above water surfaces for no apparent reason. Except that makes no sense. The thought of that frightens me. How could I even entertain such magical possibilities? I must not let my mind deceive me. I must continue.*

**U.S. DEPARTMENT OF INTELLIGENCE**


Report: AXZU, Worldwide Blackout Incident, March 14, 21**

Dated: April 1, 21**

Archive Number: ZUY-12364400____C

Name of the Civilian: [name deleted]

Age: 24

Occupation: Student

Interviewer: Lieut. Michael Jones


I was on the toilet between third and fourth period. That's when I usually have to go. Something to do with ingesting too much coffee on an empty stomach. I don't really remember nodding off, man. It was as fast as... how do they say? It happened in the blink of an eye, that fast. I didn't feel groggy or anything along the likes, I just got up, finished my business and flushed, same as usual. Except it was dark when I walked out. That's what threw me off. I couldn't even entertain the possibility of having nodded off—I would've known—, besides, I had consumed a ridiculous amount of coffee. There was no way I would've been going to sleep anytime soon. I thought, *the aliens are coming!* It was either that or some sort of government experiment, breaking the sky or something. But I tried to be realistic, so I concluded it must be an eclipse. Or something along the likes.

Then I got to class, and everyone was looking around, confused, asking questions. Maybe they hadn't heard about the eclipse. Prof. [name deleted] was trying to calm down a few of the girls, but he didn't seem to be having a good grip of the situation either. A few minutes later, he clumsily announced class was cancelled, and left in a frenzy, jacket half on. I had to ask what was up to one of the other guys. He told me we had lost five hours. I wasn't really sure what he meant until he pointed at the clock on the wall. Yeah, he was right. No wonder the Prof. was panicking. What in the world had happened? Do you guys know?

# R³

**Were you feeling any different after the incident? Any symptoms? Peculiarities?**

Not particularly. I wasn't able to get any decent shut-eye the first night, but that's because my nerves were on edge. After that, things gradually fell back on track; people went on with their lives and less and less individuals brought the event up. Even the news stopped talking about it. It felt as if they were scared or something.

**So nothing unusual with your sleep? Nothing at all?**

Well, I'm not sure how to put this…

**Do your best.**

But like... my sleep, feels... empty. I hope you don't think I'm crazy but I don't know how else to explain it. It feels different. My body isn't tired when I wake up in the morning, but it almost feels as if my brain had been unplugged during all those hours, and time had suddenly disappeared. I don't know, I guess that doesn't make any sense...

# R³

**Have you had any dreams since the incident?**

Dreams? Now that you mention it, no I haven't. Like I said, sleep was an off switch with no timeline, no dreams, no nothing. Is that happening to everyone else too?

**We can't answer that. Has anyone been around you while you slept? Or have you been around anyone sleeping?**

No, I don't think so. If I'm trying to sleep with someone, we are not usually sleeping, get what I'm saying? Ha ha ha, so no, not really.

**Thank you.**

Why? Is there something wrong with me?

## They're looking for you.

"Mr. Hammond?"

I'm standing there, holding the door open for the two dicks in suits. If I didn't know any better, I would say they never left. They somehow managed to grow roots outside my apartment door, waiting until Isaac's ghosts—or whatever that was—stepped out to say "hello".

# R³

"Mr. Hammond?" the fat one repeats.

"Yes?" I finally spit out.

"We hate to disturb you again," he lies, "but as you may know, your building manager is still missing."

"Oh, is he?" I lie.

"Yes, he is."

We all lie.

When I realize both their faces are mine. Not that they resemble mine, but that they are in fact mine. It's as if someone had magically cloned me in the last fifteen seconds, dressed my doubles in suits and conveniently positioned them outside my apartment; all part of an elaborate prank. Except they don't notice, only I do. Yet I'm not surprised. I'm not surprised to find myself facing myself, staring down at myself, lying at myself. A copy of a copy of a copy stuck in an endless loop of repeating probabilities.

"Maybe he left," I tell my copies.

"Excuse me? Left where?" asks the one copy that used to be a tall man.

"Like on vacation."

"Did he mention he was taking a vacation?"

"No."

"Did he hint on taking a vacation? Leaving town?"

"No."

# R³

"Is this based on a hunch of yours?" the one that used to be fat asks, very much irritated.

"He looked like he needed one. I don't know. I'm not a cop. Isn't that your job?" My copies exchange frustrated glances. Then bam, their faces are back to normal—back to their own average, forgettable faces.

"Thank you once again, Mr. Hammond."

I slam the door shut before they walk away.

I never get any mail, but when I do it's the usual garbage: bills, bills, bills, all past due. Every single one of them as if on cue. At least I got rent taken care off, I think as Isaac slurps his soup at the table.

"They're looking for you," I joke. He can't hear me. Or has decided to ignore me. "Should I tell them to stop looking? That they'll never find you?"

A fork randomly levitates and smashes against the wall, as if pulled by a giant magnet. Perhaps that's his way of saying "fuck off". He's been known to be a moody prick.

I stare at the fork closely as it continues to vibrate due to magnetic tension, releasing a soft but lingering hum. *What in the world is going on?*

As soon as I try to snap it off the wall, a tiny shock speeds through my right arm, pushing me back a few feet.

*Ouch.*

# $R^3$

The tips of my right hand's fingers are covered in deep black ash. I scrape some off and smell it. It smells like nothing.

Slowly, zigzagging strings of pure electricity grow out of my ashy fingertips, stretching out elegantly as would recently planted seeds, bursting through the soil, reaching out for the sun.

# THE POSTER GIRL FOR DREAMING

*October 24, 1591*

*Last night I had quite an unusual dream. For days my sleep has been light and rather dreamless, which is not often the case. It's common for me to sleep deeply, and have rather elaborate dreams. I knew the new environment would have some effect on my mind. It was expected to disturb my sleep pattern. However, I was able to recall one dream.*

*I found myself walking in an open field blanketed with pure white snow. The deep blue sky was clear, having no cloud in sight. No mountains or distinctive landmarks were discernible in a distance; only pure, spotless white. In fact, it was so vast, you could see the slight curve where sky met field on the horizon. This could've been the North Pole. It was hard to tell if there was dirt or water under the layer of ice. I walked a mile or so, before I found myself surrounded by a small patch of crystal cacti. Whether they were frozen or something else, I didn't know, but their geometry was more familiar to the crystal family than to ice. These bodies refracted light into a breathtaking spectacle. They resembled crystallized stalactites protruding from the ice block I stood on. Whether or not there were actual cacti inside was a mystery, but they resembled them in shape and pattern.*

*A distant roar echoing throughout the sky caused me to turn. The blue sky was now gone, replaced by thick dark clouds, swarmed with playful lightning bolts pulsating inside, soaking up energy, ready to attack. Wind and storm had materialized, literally out of thin air. Seeking for cover was pointless; there was no shelter visible within a five-*

# R³

*mile radius. I decided to make my way out of the crystal-cacti field, as to avoid attracting any lightning. These crystals may or may not be conduits.*

*I had made it a few yards away from the storm and crystal field, when I turned, out of pure curiosity, to watch the up-coming events—whatever those could possibly be—unfold. That's when I saw her, the woman with fiery hair. She stood in the middle of the crystal field, looking up at the storm, unnerved by its proximity. Her white gown flapped wildly, but she did not seem to care about the mighty winds. No matter how much I yelled or waved my arms, she was not able to hear me—that or she had decided to ignore me. Her eyes were fixed on the loaded clouds. After concluding she could not hear me, due to the gushing winds overpowering any other sound, I ran back towards the crystal field waving my arms up and down. Once I was less than twenty feet away, she turned in response to one of my cries. I immediately stopped, relieved. In retrospect, perhaps she only turned so I would stop running, to keep me from harm's way, as if she had known, somehow, that two seconds later a streak of light of walloping force would tear through the clouds and pierce through her body, knocking it five feet away.*

# R³

*I rapidly made way to her inanimate self, fearing lightning would strike again. The wind had mitigated to a level of stillness, revealing the roundness of her abdomen under her gown. This woman had to be at least eight months pregnant. Her eyes fluttered open as her lips parted and words weightlessly floated out.*

*When I woke up I instantly felt the words leaving my memory, laggardly withering, recoiling into the dark pits of my mind, refusing to come out to the light. And as the day went by, so did the vivid memory of my dream, but I shall not worry; as I'm sure it will come back to me in passed time.*

Steady footsteps approach the dark cavern, triggering the young man to rapidly pocket his book. A few seconds later, a man in his fifties with a white robe, a blue bowtie and glasses enters the room. His studious but friendly face reviews the data on the capsule's monitor and compares it with the notes on his clipboard. This scientist is new. The young man has never seen him down there before, at least not during his prolonged shifts. Perhaps the smelly, pudgy man got transferred, the young man hopes. The old scientist enters the sphere leaving the door open behind him.

"You can come in," he says from inside.

The young man peeks his head inside the white vault, hesitant, unsure if this is some kind of test.

The old scientist inputs a code into the touch screen by the capsule, causing the top section to slide open, leaving only a thick layer of glass between its contents and the outside world. The smelly, pudgy man had never been this friendly to him, not to mention inviting.

"Any update, Bill?" the scientist asks, in a gentle but firm voice.

The young man with rosy cheeks shakes his head from side to side, avoiding any eye contact. "How do you know my name?"

"It's on your name tag," he says with a smile. "I'm Dr. Walker. Keep a close eye on her for me, will you? She's very important to us."

Seemingly satisfied, Dr. Walker leaves. Young Bill waits a beat and then peeks out the door, making sure he's gone. Distant footsteps gradually fade into silence. He has been left alone once again, but this time inside the ominous white sphere inside the vast dark cavern; a concentrate of light trapped inside an ocean of darkness.

Young Bill approaches the incubator observing its contents for the first time: a beauty with blazing hair, in deep sleep. He's seen her on TV. He's seen her on commercials. The world knows her face. The face of R³. The poster girl for dreaming.

Nina. Why is she here?

Wires jut out of her forehead and chest. Tubes protrude from the back of her neck and arms. This incubator is feeding her; helping her breathe; keeping her alive.

How long has she been in here? There is no way of telling. Her life-support capsule is deceiving, as it is also draining her—her life is hanging by a thread.

The substance flowing out of her body and into these tubes is helping entire populations regain a sliver of what they lost after the incident, young Bill thinks. She is the Holy Grail, and Bill isn't strong enough to resist such delicious temptation. He hasn't dreamt since he was twelve. R³ never compared to the true experience. It was too processed, too watered-down, nothing like the real thing. But now, he has found the source. Raw. Pure. He could smell the possibilities, causing every bone in his body to quiver with titillation.

Not wasting another minute, he rapidly unplugs an IV, replacing it with a small, empty test tube. The tube instantly fills with a glowing yellowish serum. Nina's unseen eyes flutter rapidly.

This violates all protocol, but when faced with the genesis, the fountain of dreams, rules crumble into oblivion.

# R³

The security, the elevators, the underground facility; it all makes sense. They are attempting to protect the most treasured faculty human lives currently lack: dreaming. He can get fired for this. Face serious jail time. Even get killed, but it is all worth it.

Once the tube is full—all ten milliliters—, young Bill replaces the IV and turns to her, giving this god-like creature one last look: no motion, only deep, uncharted sleep.

He wonders what she is dreaming about? The feral worlds housed inside her subconscious. Untamed. Free.

He corks the tube and leaves.

In the middle of the night, parked in an empty lot, young Bill jumps into the back of his van, rolls up his sleeve and lays on a make-shift bed. He drains the glowing, yellowish serum out of the test tube with a syringe, and injects it directly into his bloodstream. The moment it hits his system, Bill begins to twitch violently, letting out a painful groan. His eyes tighten shut, as tiny, fluid specks of light flicker over the vault of his eyelids. Cell-like. They float around other microorganisms of various sizes. There's one main cell pulsating to his heartbeat. The liquid around it suddenly perforates the membrane—violated—, quickly intertwining with the cell's contents.

Young Bill tries to relax but he can't control it. Every muscle group contracts as the fluid consumes his body. Suddenly his eyes shoot to the back of his head and he collapses. He stops moving.

Air lightly wheezes out of his relaxed jaw.

Images flip like a slide show through the visual innards of his brain.

An indescribable level of joy overpowers Bill's pleasure core, as Nina, on a swing, laughs hysterically, full of life. Her untamable hair breezes in and out of her face, as she runs up a meadow, with knee-high sunflowers swaying at her every move. She drops on her back, in a fit of melodic giggles, orgasmic music to Bill's ears.

Back in the van, young Bill starts convulsing. Memory lane takes a sharp turn as a doctor examines Nina's vitals. There's something wrong. Her skin is flushed, her face is gaunt. Her kaleidoscopic eyes tear up in fear, as the color slowly fades out of them. A large capsule envelops her like an embryo. Droning hums reverb inside her ears, forcing electrical stimuli into her delicate brain. Bright lights— flash, flash, flash—rupture her dilated pupils. She can't breathe. The capsule rapidly collapses around her, victim to an intense claustrophobia attack. The doctors monitor her every move, unnerved, standing in a chamber labeled *Under Observation*. She slams her tiny hands and feet against the inner walls, but the smooth, white fiberglass secures her in.

Young Bill convulses. His face rapidly pixelates; pieces shift like a live jigsaw puzzle, turning and flipping, shooting and swirling like intertwining constellations of light, slowly morphing into John Hammond's face. His head bangs violently on the van's floor, over and over again. A heartbeat later, a dry exhale wheezes out of his lips as young Bill's face switches back to normal. His body stops moving. His eyes fall into deep sleep. His breathing returns to normal. Yet he is far from normality.

**THE YEAR OF THE NOW**

Haggard Bill creeps into the run-down locker room, scanning the perimeter making sure he wasn't followed. He pushes his stringy, gray hair back and goes to the locker marked "314", punches in the code, and opens it. He stands motionless.

As expected, the locker is empty. Color bleeds from Bill's worn out face, as he closes the metallic door. He doesn't understand why. He doesn't understand how John was able to find the R³. How could he have known?

# R³

Something shifts inside him. Not willing to accept the reality of his current situation, he reopens the locker. Yet nothing changes; once again, he finds himself face-to-face with the empty locker—pure, clean emptiness. The void eats him up inside. He closes it, then opens it, then closes it again, and reopens it—repeatedly, as if expecting the bottle to somehow reappear, but it's not there. His repetitive opening and closing grows louder and louder and louder and louder.

Until reality forces itself upon him.

He slams it shut.

## *Unus Mundus.*

Dr. Hammond's eyes are wide open, motionless—a still life capturing the equally numbing and despairing quality of sleep: serene, disturbing, mocking the stillness of death.

An alarm goes off and his chest slowly rises, as oxygen flutters in and out of his nostrils. His eyes roll up towards the back of his head, following with a gentle couple of blinks. Suddenly animated, he rises. Unlike most of the rest of the population, Dr. Hammond has never ingested a snowflake. Its properties were engineered to cover more than achieving pleasantness and "eye-shut-sleep". In a way, that is the façade highlighted in the pool of chemicals that comprise the snowflake. Listed as secondary effects, you will find: "numbness, possible short-term memory loss, disorientation, decrease in brain wave production"—many of these are simply overlooked by those who, above all, want to feel 'good', no matter how sedated it will make them in the long run. The complete opposite of what R³ had intended.

The first hues of breaking morning filter through his bathroom window as he showers, letting the water douse him completely, eyes wide shut, resembling a purifying ceremony.

The sharp blade glides steadily across his rugged face, a tight grip skimming across his neck, kissing his jugular—precision and order, the core foundation of his morning routine.

The perfectly iron pressed shirt slides with ease up his toned arms. He buttons up with surgical care. The dark blue slacks slip on, tightening firmly around the waist. His closet holds rows of identical combinations. His polished shoes slip on without aid. The alarm clock on his nightstand reads: 6:20 AM.

The doorbell rings.

# R³

Dr. Hammond signs for a package and rolls in a wooden crate the size of a chair on a dolly. A label on the side reads *FRAGILE*.

A workstation has been set up in the middle of his garage. No car in sight. The empty crate, overflowing with Styrofoam stuffing, sits on the floor. Wearing protective gloves and an air mask, Dr. Hammond hits a nail onto a wooden board with a hammer. There's an unidentifiable object attached to the wooden base.

In the bathroom, he scrubs his hands repeatedly, using a special antibacterial soap. Suddenly, he's caught in the firing range of his empty reflection. He feels "off", as if there was something different with his face. As if it had changed shape overnight and he had failed to notice. He splashes some water and rubs his temples—it feels as if he is rubbing someone else's face.

I feel Dr. Hammond's gaze looming over me as I lie on the Chaise Lounge. I'm sure he's thinking how frazzled I look. Can't blame him. This is slowly eating me up inside, hitting a brick wall over and over again, finding no way out or through. Also I think his office got bigger. That's probably impossible, but I'm certain it's bigger.

"That wasn't her dream," I say. "I was in there too, it was *our* dream. I feel she's living inside me now. Like she's part of me."

# R³

"You can feel her pain," Dr. Hammond says before removing his glasses and rubbing the bridge of his nose. "Do you think it's possible to have a collective dream?" he asks after a brief pause.

"Isn't that why they made Nina's Dream? So everyone could have the same dream?"

"When I say 'collective dreams', think of them as a pool, a large preexisting pool of water where all possible dreams are drawn from. Similar to Carl Jung's 'collective unconscious'. Are you familiar with Jung?"

I have no idea who the fuck he's talking about.

"In a nutshell, he believed there existed a collective and universal second consciousness, which was identical in all individuals. In this hypothetical dream pool, the combinations are infinite. Your dream is only an extension of that pool. A stream born out of that pool. Or a branch, extending from a very large tree. A *Unus Mundus*."

"A what?"

"An underlying unified reality where everything emerges from and returns to. But since no one dreams anymore, why say no to the possibility that you had a dream someone else already had? Or a dream someone else is having at the exact same time allowing you to somehow connect with them?"

"Or perhaps I'm swimming against the current... Heading back towards the large pool... towards the magical lake..." I add, not sure why.

112

# R³

"What if we all were part of the same entity, with different points of view, with personalized realities? Branches off a tree. In a way, living the same thing. One consciousness experiencing itself subjectively."

"I don't think we are all living the same thing."

He stares at me intensely. "Does this bother you?"

"It sounds like you're trying to make your life meaningful."

"You think life has no meaning?"

"I think you were born to die."

"What makes you say that?"

"Don't you feel cheated? Being born..." I pause, for dramatic effect, and then add, "...without the ability to dream?"

He takes a moment, making an effort to digest this. "Do you think we are all entitled to dream?"

"You're like a race horse with limited vision. Do you think it's a coincidence our names are exactly the same, yet we're not related? An astronomic joke somehow stating we are the same person?"

"I do think it's a coincidence. Do you think it could be more than a random occurrence? Meeting by chance?"

*The universe happened by chance.*

"This world is a metaphor," I say.

"A metaphor for what?"

# R³

"Ever since that dream, I wake up every morning with the same feeling that everything is suddenly speeding up—rushing towards one destination."

The metallic object cuts through the space-like environment, faster and faster.

I can feel it. *It's approaching.*

"Are your parents alive?" I'm not sure why, but I felt like asking.

"We are here for you John, but if it helps, yes, they are," Dr. Hammond replies.

"I meant your real parents. BI-O-LO-GI-CAL. Did you ever meet your mother? Could she dream?" *How do I know this?* I'm not sure exactly what, or who, has taken over me.

This strikes a chord in Dr. Hammond, yet he hides it very well. He doesn't answer. Instead, his energy is driven towards grabbing a small, porcelain teakettle from a side table. It's simple and elegant, adorned with a Fleur-de-lis pattern.

"Would you like some tea?" he asks.

Is this a test? "No".

Dr. Hammond pours tea into a large cup. He takes a small sip. It's hot. He blows the steam off gently. His body flow has suddenly changed. The way he moves has become elastic and unsettling. He takes another sip and releases a pleased "mm", happier with the temperature. Seemingly content, he proceeds.

"Please, tell me more about your dream."

The atmosphere in the room drops, as if we had suddenly descended miles and miles deep, to somewhere underground.

I let his question sink in. Not sure why, but I find myself incredibly uncomfortable and annoyed. Every little sip Dr. Hammond takes becomes loud and irritating. I can feel myself grimace at every instance.

"I need to find this woman," I finally say.

"Right, from your dream." Sip. Sip.

Annoyed, I glare. "Yes—from my dream. She can fix this. Bring everything back to normal."

"But John, what is *normal?*"

Dr. Hammond nonchalantly dips his small tea plate into the teacup, as if dunking a cracker. Immediately after, he takes a large bite off the plate and chews loudly.

*Very* loudly.

The grinding bites my ear ducts.

A few splinters—crumbs?—land on his nicely pressed shirt. He licks his fingers and retrieves a napkin. For whatever reason, I find this incredibly annoying and rude. How dare he eat during my session? Not only is he eating, but he is eating loudly; it's incredibly distracting.

# R³

"I apologize. I thought I could hold off until lunch, but I couldn't."

I squirm along willingly as he escorts me out of his office. Torture is finally over. The grinding seemed to have gone on forever. In my case, things only keep heading south.

My mother, applying a bold red lipstick, sits at the edge of a designer chair in the waiting room. She playfully clicks her compact mirror shut at the sight of us, releasing in excitement, what one can only describe as an exotic bird's mating shrill.

"Oooooooooeeeeh!!"

She's unusually dolled up, having graduated from the mumu into more fitting—yet incredibly tacky—clothing. Her make-up is intense, as if she had stepped out of a surreal 1980's soap. Did she lose weight? Since yesterday?

"Sweet bug! What a lovely surprise!" she wails—*please, kill me now*. "How's he doing, doctor? Isn't he a good boy?"

It's one of those moments of real-life slow-motion, where even though things take longer to occur, you are helpless to the events, unable to stop the impending result. A wet, lipstick-infused kiss lands on my cheek, and there is nothing I can do about it. I instantly wipe it off after the fact.

# R³

"I had no idea he was your son," he lies. All lies. "Why, you could be his slightly older sister."

*Kill me now.*

*Now. Now. Now. Now.*

"Oh, doctor Hammond!"

A heinous act of mutual verbal masturbation. Bile rises to my mouth. I swallow. My mother's attention instantly shifts, as she squints her eyes trying to scan the inner sanctity of Dr. Hammond's perfect pores.

"Oh my! You have lovely skin. Doesn't he have lovely skin?" she asks an invisible figure standing somewhere between us. "I had never noticed it before."

"I moisturize," he says, showcasing his perfectly white TV advertisement teeth. "Are you ready for your session?"

Do they even know I'm here? I'm afraid they'll start dry humping. Scratch that: terrified. That could scar me for life. God, he could be her son...

"Been looking forward to it! I have so much to tell you."

And with that, they both disappear inside the office, completely forgetting about my troubled, pathetic self. I wipe my cheek again.

*Sick.*

## *Our reality is slowly collapsing.*

I get lost inside my InstaMeal reflection. Again.

The soup is untouched, probably cold. I wonder what's going on down there? Inside my reflection... on the other side...

My thoughts have been trailing off into similar tangents lately. I find myself fixating on random objects —more like

# R³

fixating on the space *around* those objects—for hours. My mind rockets off to some uncharted territory, returning several moments later. It would be fantastic if I could remember most of these mindless travels, but like a self-destructive mechanism with a Swiss clock design, it obliterates itself completely the second it returns to its departure point, usually triggered by my itch.

Oh yeah, I forgot to mention, my head has been itching at uncontrollable levels. I thought about getting some lice shampoo but it's only on one particular spot, so it might be a mosquito bite, which makes little sense, since it's not mosquito weather, but what do I know? It's a bug; bug does what it wants.

Isaac walks past me, leaving a trail of air ripples behind. I don't have to look; I can sense them behind me. It's a little game we play. A little game. That's all this is.

I slowly lift my hand and *poke* the air. It ripples as if it were made out of jell-o. A light-hearted scoff slips out of my lips. I stare at the emptiness, amused.

Trying to mimic Isaac, I *pinch* the air with both hands and pull, dragging the streak of color strings towards the center. I form a teapot. A white, porcelain teapot with a blue Fleur-de-lis design. Similar to Dr. Hammond's, except mine is rather shapeless—like a deformed child imitating reality. It immediately shatters, mid-air.

# R³

*Drip, drip;* a thin stream of blood trickles down my nose. I dab it with my fingers, wondering how this came about. I don't remember snorting any coke.

Like shifting engines, my entire apartment goes dark as a deep-seated hum decays with a quick decrescendo. The same thing happens with the AC. Even silence grows quiet.

I flick the lighter on my right hand, allowing it to burn faintly. Isaac sits across from me, obviously annoyed by our current situation. He's the roommate I never wanted; takes up space, eats my food, and doesn't pay rent. You could say the fact he works for the building changes things a bit, but it still doesn't give him the right. It's a matter of principle. He is gloom personified.

*You're in a mood. I can't stay here.*

It must've been two in the morning when I got to Bill's.

"You look like shit," he says. "Have you slept?"

"Thanks."

As I walk across the RV, I can't help but notice the floor is moving—breathing—as an unusual sea of people lie sprawled across cushions and blankets on the floor; a human minefield. Trying not to step on them is painstakingly hard. They are sleeping, smoking, eating, all with hazy eyes. Bill drags me towards the only loitering-free corner.

"What's with the crashers?" I ask.

# R³

"They're friends. They all want to dream. Like you, John."

"Right. Bill, something weird is happening."

"Yes, yes. You're absolutely right. Something *is* happening. After our last talk I couldn't wrap my head around it but then I realized—when you drank the R³, you unlocked something... you became her vessel."

"Her?"

"Nina's. You're the vessel, John. The umbilical cord connecting us to her." Bill's eyes seem like they're about to pop out of their orbits. He rarely blinks. His passion is somewhat terrifying. "John, you're the burnt bridge that once connected all of us to the subconscious, to the dream world. We are waiting for that bridge to be rebuilt. We are waiting to cross that bridge. But we have to leave soon, John. Time is of utter importance."

"Why?"

"John, this world will shatter. Our reality is slowly collapsing, like a dead tree cut off from its nutrients." Bill looks around and adds in an unusual, secretive mode: "I have something to show you."

We walk into the only sectioned-off part of the RV: his bedroom; a six-by-nine rectangle with an old cot stuck in a corner and no walking room to spare. Light doesn't seem to be a problem, as Christmas lights crawl up the walls, like firefly vines—if such a thing truly existed. They all bloom from out of a corner, in which a makeshift shrine has been set up, incorporating candles and incense. The ultimate fire hazard.

On top rests a spherical metallic object the size of a basketball. An unusual contraption resembling a satellite or *Star Wars' Death Star*, with additional worn out friezes wrapped around its surface, and a serial number etched on a strip marking its circumference.

"This will show us the answer," Bill says, admiring the object with burning desire.

I get chills.

"And then we must cross to another reality," he adds. "Only then will we become one again. And once the absolute is found, once the all-seeing-eye is born, we will all be able to dream again."

*We will be able to dream again...*

If only my dreaming would stop...


I curl up as much as the cot allows, eyes wide open, unable to sleep. It's incredibly uncomfortable, but I don't mind. I've slept on harder surfaces. Bill sits on a large pile of pillows at the end of the cot, smoking out of a large pipe, attached to one of those electronic Hookahs. Smoke slithers in and out of his nostrils, spreading everywhere as he sways back and forth with his eyes closed, humming, while rubbing the metallic sphere. The tune becomes increasingly familiar. The instrument is different—not a jingle, but a hum. It's the same melody that keeps visiting my brain, forcefully drilling itself in, branding all my senses with who knows what.

Nausea suddenly fills my insides, wreaking havoc. I blame the Hookah. But I know it's the jingle. Unable to take it, I get up and leave.

## *Gregor Samsa.*

My eyelids weigh a hundred tons. Did someone glue them shut? Liquid oozes out of my chapped lips, and hangs like a static pendulum fed off inertia. It's sticky.

Pushing myself back on my knees proves to be incredibly difficult. My arms are either extremely weak, or my body has grown three times heavier. I feel like a disproportionate bug. *Gregor Samsa* on his worst of days. Mutating. The bathtub has become my bed, back to the womb. If only I could remember how I got here, or how this blanket made its way on me.

I itch my head. Hard. It's been happening in spurts—the itching, that is. I completely forget about it, until it happens. I can feel my imperfect nails burying into my scalp, moving back and forth, minimizing the itch, replacing it only with a numbing sensation.

I don't recognize my hands. They look like the crypt keeper's hands, yet somehow they are attached to my alien body. There's dry blood buried under my nails. How hard was I scratching?

I gag, thinking I'm about to throw up, but Isaac is using the toilet seat as a thinking chair. He raises his hand and presses his bony index finger against his thin, dry lips.

"Shhhh…"

A few pots and pans bounce off the kitchen floor, rattling loudly.

*Who else is here?*

We are not alone. I know that for a fact, as I get closer to the kitchen. Perhaps I forgot to lock my door on my way in. Maybe I'm getting ransacked, not that there's much to ransack.

But alas, no ransacking. Worse. My mother.

# R³

She goes through the cabinets and fumbles with the stove. She smacks it, frustrated. She pops a snowflake pill in an attempt to relax, I assume. Breathes. In. And out.

"What are you doing?" I mumble.

Her bones jump out of her skin as she drops pots and pans again—*claaaaank! Clank!* Claaank!! *Fucking clank....*

"Sweet bug!" she shrieks, and then takes (yet another) deep breath. "You're finally awake. You weren't answering my calls. I got worried."

"They cut the phone line."

"And your power," she adds. "I wanted to make you breakfast but you have no power, John. You have no power," she firmly says, her eyes widening like an irate Shih Tzu.

What did she mean by that? *No power?*

I step on an old syringe. Suddenly I snap out of my stupor, mauled by the elephant in the room. My pills, pipes, powders, all scattered over the counters, like bread crumbs left behind in an attempt to find my way back into Wonderland. I shove them all into a drawer. She pretends not to notice, but this time she's not very good at it. I can feel myself getting aggravated, feeling intruded, invaded, my face boiling red, my eyes tearing up, and my eyelids growing even heavier.

"What are you doing??!" I snap, frustrated.

A small, but firm slap propels my face from right to left.

# R³

"You have no power, John!" she barks back. "You need to fix it! You look like hell." The poisonous tone in her voice throws me back. Did a gorgon take over? What's with this sudden explosion of sternness? She's morphing...

Like me.

Like *Samsa*.

Her demeanor instantly changes, her pleasant smile returning, the dark pits in her eyes fading away.

"Your drawings!" she wails, suddenly remembering as she digs through her purse. "I found them when I was cleaning the closet. Aren't they adorable? They're some of the first you ever did."

She slaps the whole set of about ten drawings, made by a five-year-old with heavy Crayola, onto my hands. I flip through them, quickly noticing they all portray a tall woman with red hair and shimmering eyes—*kaleidoscopic* even.

"Look how tall you drew me! My little artist," her words trail off into white noise as I recede into the depths of my broken brain.

That's not her.

That's Nina.

# *Has somebody else been living my life all this time?*

I don't know how long it's been, but I'm out of breath from my constant pacing back and forth. Dr. Hammond observes the drawings closely as I try to make sense of all this nonsense, like trying to wrap a mountain with a candy-wrapper.

# R³

"It's her! Nina! The woman I met that night. I've met her before," I say before I catch sight of myself on a reflective surface; my eyes are incredibly bloodshot. Dr. Hammond rubs his chin. I finally drop into the couch like a ton of bricks.

"Don't you see it?" I ask.

His lively eyes leave the drawings and focus on me, studying me like an oil painting, choosing his words carefully, picking them with tweezers from the word bank in his brain.

"John, how old would you say the woman in your drawings is?"

I know where this is going. "Twenty. Maybe twenty-five."

"How old was the woman you met that night?"

*Same age.* I bury my head between my hands, feeling suddenly defeated, rubbing my eyes, my temples, my entirety.

"Isn't it possible that your meeting with this woman was only a product of your brain, your memories, triggered by the R³ you drank?"

*No. No. No.* I can feel my self-assurance crushing my defeat.

"She was real. As real as you, as real as me. As real as this couch, as real as this office."

"These hallucinogens have clouded your brain, warped your reality."

# R³

I grasp at straws. "If our realities are based on—on the inner workings of our brains, right? Wouldn't that make what's real, relative?"

"John, there's no tangible proof you actually met this woman that night," he shuts me down.

"I slept with her! I know I slept with her! Jesus! Fuck!"

"You said you met her after being greatly intoxicated. You're the best example of an 'unreliable narrator'. You imagined everything."

"No I didn't! I remember saving her."

"Saving her from what?"

I look up, confused. What's going on in my brain? I'm pulling on all these threads, pulling and pulling, thinking they're leading me somewhere, when all of a sudden, a tall brick wall. Dead end. "I don't know. In another life?"

Dr. Hammond removes his glasses and rubs his temples, letting out a small sigh in despair. I notice for the first time how alike we look. Something in the way we deal with dejection. A slight resemblance... yet it's gone as swiftly as it appears. I believe this man genuinely wants to help, but he doesn't know how.

"There's one way..." he begins, "to find out... to be somewhat certain... if this is true or not..." He looks up, setting off dramatic drum rolls, "by digging up your first encounter with this woman."

"What's that?"

# R³

"It's quite an ancient tool, actually. Since the day people stopped dreaming, it didn't seem to work anymore, but you're—well, *different*. Would you be willing to try hypnosis?"

It sounds familiar. "Will that show you my memories?"

"You will provide me access to your subconscious. Maybe even access to secrets you've been keeping from yourself. The mind is strewn with hidden rooms and boxes, all with their own protective combinations. If we are lucky, we might find the source of your nightmare. If we don't, we try something else. You have nothing to lose."

"How do we do it?"

"First, we put you to sleep."

I lie on the faint couch, controlling my breathing as indicated. He tells me to close my eyes. I do.

"As I count down to zero," he says, "you will reach a state of deep sleep. No wall will remain up." *That would be a first.* He continues in a soothing, monotonous voice. "They'll unfold like windows allowing a pleasant summer breeze through. Ten," he begins. "Nine. Eight. Seven. Six. Five. Four. Three. Two. One."

Eyes snap open. Seconds later they roll to the back of the head. I float up and above, becoming a fly in the vast room, looking down suspended mid-air. Below, Dr. Hammond lays on the chaise lounge I had previously occupied, asleep.

# R³

But he isn't himself. He's me. Or at least looks like me. His face is gaunt, hair short, and wears my exact same clothes.

My floating self is led towards the other end of the room, towards the leather chair where Dr. Hammond had previously been sitting. In his place, conveniently dressed in nice slacks and shiny shoes, is... *me*. Clean-cut. Sharp. Even handsome. Somewhat resembling Dr. Hammond, but me...

Our bodies have inexplicably switched, instantly accepting our new reality as true.

"Any remaining walls will crumble at the snap of my fingers," I continue the process Dr. Hammond started, taking his place on the chair.

"Five. Four. Three. Two..."

*Snap*. My thumb and middle finger sing once the proper friction is applied. It echoes loudly.

"From this point on," I say calmly, "identity becomes an illusion."

And that's when the night terrors start and everything truly heads south.

Dressed in Dr. Hammond's perfectly pressed shirt, I tweak the last details of his machine—small and spherical. Thin tubes come out of it. It looks like a brewing device. Except

# R³

it's attached to a larger object resembling an incubator; like an iron lung. I'm in his garage.

I have no idea what this device is, but somehow I know how to put it together. I am blind software acting on some else's hardware. Sleepwalking.

*Who am I? Am I him? Am I me? Who is me?*

*Has somebody else been living my life all this time?*

I feel like myself, yet the basic mechanics I follow are not mine, as if my lips were moving, but the voice slipping out and the words forming were alien.

I place the hammer on the work table, next to the rolled up plans and diagrams. I feel satisfied with the result. A sign meaning my work is done. I roll up my right sleeve and insert an IV gently. Next, a long thin needle goes straight into the base of my head, where skull meets the neck. The droning sound begins once I switch the device on. It means it's working.

From inside the incubator, a glowing, yellowish serum pours out and in through a tube into the newly constructed brewing machine. Like a dialysis, it seems to break the serum down, filtering it through an even thinner tube that feeds both into my arm and brain.

I find myself floating above it all again; a fly on the wall. I have a hard time drawing a line as to when these occurrences begin and end. There's no longer black or white, only gray.

# R³

I fly towards the other end of the room—towards the large incubator that feeds off the serum.

Inside the incubator I find myself. Not Dr. Hammond, as myself, but my actual self, in deep, deep sleep, a result of his deep hypnosis. *Is he draining me? How did I get here?*

Paralyzed. Frozen. Lifeless.

Until I see my eyes flutter.

Fluttering rapidly.

Dreaming.


*It means it's working.*

# TWO

## WHERE DID HER DREAMS GO?

*November 24, 1591*

*After a thirty-one day journey, I came across a village, small in size; a community made-up of four to five single story homes, a barn and a well. They're all family folk, farmers constantly catering to their land. When I asked for directions to the nearest town, they gaped at me with curious confusion, as if they hadn't understood what I'd said. I repeated the question only to be told they didn't know. They seldom interacted with strangers outside their community. They had settled into this particular area years back and hadn't left since. They rarely had visitors; more like wondering travelers who had lost their way. Some decided to stay, as new additions to their community, others went back on their journeys. I thanked them for their generosity as they fed me and offered lodging, but I had to be on my way. Once again they grew confused, as if unsure of where exactly was I planning on returning to. Nonetheless, they kindly provided me with food supplies, and offered me a horse to facilitate my travels. A little boy brought me a young steed from their barn. The beast rose on its hind legs the moment I approached it, probably reacting in terror. The boy grabbed the beast's head gently. It immediately calmed down and lowered its head. The boy pressed his forehead against the beast's, while caressing it's mane. Only then, did the horse allow me to approach it and climb on its back. It had become a different creature before my own eyes. This boy possessed some kind of magic. "Magic"... I found myself lost at words, unable to find a logical explanation. That is when I stopped, I stopped trying; I stopped looking. If logic wanted to be found, then it would reveal itself, once the time was right; not a moment sooner, not a moment later.*

*I set off, resuming my journey, hoping my intuition would guide me to the closest town in a manner similar to the way it had lead me to this welcoming village.*

*November 30, 1591*

*I have managed to cover more terrain with the help of this loyal steed, than I was able to explore by foot during those thirty-one days. Even so, we have yet to come across any other settlement. Whichever way I go, I find myself running into denser forests with waist-high greenery, growing into walls of impenetrable, interwoven vines and trees. I'm low on supplies. If I'm unable to find a settlement before the next sundown I will be forced to return to the community and restock.*

# R³

Young Bill stands firmly behind Dr. Walker, who reviews a thick patient file. He swims, back and forth, through a handful of pages and charts, unhappy with the results on an MRI.

"She doesn't dream anymore," he says as he rubs his temples.

"But she's in deep REM sleep. Where did her dreams go? Where are they now?" Young Bill asks, suddenly grave at the implications.

"Wherever they are, they're not here anymore. Pity. Time to pull the plug."

"Does that mean it's over? What about the R³? What about dreaming?" Bill mutters, chocking up.

"She's no longer of use to us, that's for sure. But don't worry. There'll be more. They'll find their way. They always do."

"You're going to let them dispose of her? Just like that?" he blurts out, knowing he's overstepping his grounds.

Dr. Walker freezes on the spot. An unexpected sadness seeps through his aged face, instantly disarming Bill. He can't explain what it is, but there's a certain understanding, a certain sharing of mutual disappointment at the face of this forlorn world. Shaking his head, he clears his throat and adjusts his blue bowtie before dropping a heavy red stamp on his file, DEMATERIALIZE, and leaves without saying a word.

# $R^3$

The room is suddenly quiet, except for the incubator's artificial breathing. Bill looks into the capsule—Nina's soothing beauty. Pity takes over his face. This is far beyond losing $R^3$, far beyond dreaming; he has made an actual connection with her subconscious, and he has felt her pain—a long enduring pain deeply buried beneath a hull of unnatural sleep. Feeling responsible for her, he presses his hand against the glass, longing for physical contact.

It all happens in a flash. Wide awake, Nina jolts up, her hand instantly glued against his on the glass, her face distorted with pain as her lips curl up into a muted cry for help.

His vision suddenly clouds as an infinite sequence of bursts illuminate his inner world—images juxtaposed over images at full blazing speed; images of events he's already seen; images of events he has yet to experience.

*You know what you have to do*, her haunting voice echoes inside his head.

As quick as they started, the visions are gone. Bill is suddenly launched against the spherical wall, repelled by an electric shock. He releases a groan upon impact. Stunned beyond belief, he gets up and checks on the capsule: Nina sleeps, motionless. Her vitals are down, as they were a minute ago. Shaking, he grabs the walkie-talkie, ready to call out for help. Yet he stops. *Help for what?* he thinks, cold sweat dampening his armpits. Bill breathes hard, unable to make the call. He frowns, looks hard into her still body—*was that real?* Could he be losing his mind?

He looks around and spots a silver card on the floor—a misplaced silver card key. He immediately lowers the talkie. *He must've dropped it on his way out*, he thinks.

This was his chance. There was no other way.

He knew what he had to do.

He had to save her.

## *Bill.*

I met Bill at my old job at the InstaMeal Drive-Thru. I had been there for about three weeks and I was already entertaining thoughts of suicide. Literally entertaining them. I got a few laughs by coming up with the most *out there* suicide attempts, or the bloodiest, hoping to leave a brutal mess behind for these assholes to clean. Yet, I'm currently not President of the World for that same reason. I wasn't motivated enough and every attempt fell through.

Until Bill showed up.

He stood out like a sore thumb. Nothing to do with his hippie-ish, New Age look, or rainbow flared shirt; it was the fact that he didn't have a car. At a drive-thru. I thought, hey, maybe this is his way of defying society and whatever the norm is by not having a vehicle. I even thought, good for you, I respect you, old man. But it wasn't as romantic as I had imagined. He wasn't an anarchist or a rebellious fighting force; I found this out weeks later. He simply didn't have a car. He was doing a *walk*-thru.

I didn't bother asking the first time. Last thing you want to do is engage with any potentially crazy or homeless individual. Aside from lagging in the line of cars, they usually don't order anything; just ask a series of random questions. I wish I could remember some. But I don't. I remember Bill.

He ordered food and asked to use the bathroom. This wasn't surprising, as I had the graveyard shift—I liked it better, less of a rowdy crowd, more of the silent night owls eager for a late snack. I figured he'd been out partying and needed a place to piss—and eat, of course.

It wasn't until the third night that I realized he was doing more than that. After eating his usual number 7, he'd go into the facility, into the private restroom, and relief

# R³

himself. But it didn't quite end there. Post-piss, he'd shape the food container and napkins into a makeshift pillow, and then he'd lie on it and pass out... my guess waking up around six or seven in the morning when the rush hour folks started piling in.

On that third night he had forgotten to lock the door, involuntary causing another customer to shriek in panic at the sight of him. That's when we found him; curled up on the floor, holding his sad little napkin pillow.

He later told me he had no place to stay, as I had been forced to ask him to leave. I couldn't help but feel sorry for the guy, but there was not much I could do. Can't sleep in the shitter.

He started rambling about how he had been kicked out of his apartment for having *an unlawful amount of narcotics under his possession*. I asked him what he meant by *narcotics*. I thought perhaps he was hoarding snowflakes, but those are hardly illegal, they are so legal they practically shove them down your throat.

He didn't tell me. He showed me.

I hadn't seen those little capsules or powders before. I didn't really get what he was saying when he called them *drugs*—or believed him for that matter. I only really knew of the snowflake. It didn't take much convincing for me to try a handful of whatever he fed me. Next thing I knew, I was inviting him to crash on my couch.

And that's how this beautiful friendship was born.

# R³

A week or so later, he found himself a microscopic studio apartment. However, that didn't work out either. He got evicted after two months. Tired of dealing with deposits and general landlord bullshit, he said *fuck this shit, man*, and bought himself an RV. It was his way of defying society. In that sense, I guess I was proud.

We got along pretty smoothly. Soon after I quit my job at the InstaMeal Drive-Thru—something about an incident concerning me pissing in the soda fountain, *allegedly*—we started hanging out 24/7. He had an endless supply of stories. He told me how he lost his arm; something to do with a door accident, and how he hates children—more like, *they make me uncomfortable; I'm never certain what's going on behind those empty eyes*.

He used to be a lab tech, got fired, lost everything. He became a hermit, living off what the street provided, seeking shelter inside a sewer here and there. But whatever horrors he witnessed during the day, were made up for at night, when he dreamt. He told me about his R³ fueled dreams. I was instantly fascinated. I loved all the narcotics he provided—every week there was something new—, but I couldn't keep my mind away from R³. It kept calling me. It became a fixation. Bill seemed reluctant to help me find any, assuring me that they had stopped making them years ago, and that by now every single bottle had been most certainly consumed. *No one would sit on dreaming for that*

# R³

*long*, he'd say.

Everything changed, however, the day I found the bottle inside the locker.

Still not sure how it happened, or the significance of it, but it's almost as if it had been calling me from miles away—whispering sweet nothings into my ear.

I didn't find that bottle.

That bottle found me.

*Not safe outside. Stay inside. Inside.*
*Inside. Safe inside.*

A dry, firm slam wakes me up. Wakes me up from what? Not sure. I rise. Every inch of my body aches, as if the tap dancing Olympics had spent all night practicing for opening ceremony on my every muscle and head. I'm running out of words to describe it. Its day-to-day continuity makes it a daily occurrence—my new status quo. If only... But the

# R³

pain increases day after day, as if someone, somewhere, were turning on a tiny, little knob every twenty-four hours, adding onto my pain, and snickering while doing so. I imagine some sort of elf or midget creature. The kind you find on cereal boxes.

I get to my front door—finally. It was no easy task. At the opposite end of it, I find a neatly taped EVICTION notice. Whoever left it must've been in a hurry because there is nobody in sight. No steps echoing down the hall.

It looks like the building is under new management. No one told me. Or perhaps this was their way of telling me. Cheeky.

Isaac has decided to take a walk on my ceiling, as if gravity had shifted but only for him. He always had an upside-down view of the world, so I guess this makes it right. Or as right as *right* can be, if that makes any sense. I realize it doesn't.

*I mustn't leave.*

*Not safe outside.*

*Stay inside.*

*Inside. Inside. Inside.*

*Safe inside.*

My fridge is empty. Why am I surprised?

*Mmm. No grubby-dubby.*

*Stomach songs want the grubby-dubby.*

*The dead one ate it all.*

He slurps his soup soundly, in his upside-down world. Has he been refilling bowl after bowl after bowl?

Stomach rumbles.

No matter how hard or which way I turn the silver knob, nothing comes out. None of them spit out what I want. I keep trying all of them: kitchen sink, bathroom sink—hoping maybe one will magically douse me with crisp liquid, like an oasis in the middle of the desert.

Nope. Nada. Zilch.

Only nasty sputters, like a war soldier chocking on his own blood.

Forgetting about my desperate need for water, I get lost in my reflection. My head itches terribly. I lower my head, hoping to find the source of such insatiable itchiness, but can only see what looks like a minor rash. That would've solved the mystery if it weren't for the amount of dark, dry blood I keep finding under my fingernails.

My teeth grind, like churning wheels at an old rusty factory, forcing out a semblance of a smile. It looks... normal. Smacking my tongue against my teeth doesn't do much in the hygiene department, but I choose to believe it does.

*Choose.*

There's something stuck in the back of my mouth, possibly between my large molars. My tongue won't bend that far back, so I stick both thumb and middle finger in an attempt of manual extraction. It's really in there. With some difficulty, I'm able to finally wrap my fingers around it and yank the nuisance out.

I squint my eyes and let out a small giggle. You'll have to admit this is rather funny. I bring my bloody tooth up close, examining its inner contours. What a curious shape they have. I'm surprised I was able to pull it out with such ease, seeing how deep the roots go. Perhaps some roots are simply not strong enough.

I dig my fingers back into my mouth, setting off exploration *Phase 2*. Middle finger and thumb wrap around another foreign object and yank it out with as much ease. Another tooth.

What do I do with two bloody teeth sitting on my hand?

*Grubby-dubby grinders for green paper?*

As a soft scoff slips out from between my lips, my reflection reaches out of the mirror with menacing arms, ready to strangle me.

Ten to fifteen people form a half circle around Bill. He smokes heavily out of his electronic Hookah, letting thin layers of smoke envelope him. The half circle of heads around him chant in unison under some sort of spell. Was it always like this? I vaguely remember the crowdedness, but the chanting doesn't strike me as familiar. However, the melody does…

*That forsaken jingle.*

Why does it follow me?

Bill's RV is certainly a bit more crowded than usual; I can smell it. Plus the new set of Christmas lights hanging from the ceiling make it impossible to walk without crouching—terrible sense of decoration.

Like some sort of self-appointed messiah, Bill sits on top of a mountain of cushions, with his right hand on the metallic sphere with odd inscriptions. The *thing* was supposed to give him all the answers, but had yet to say a word.

At the far end of the room, I spot my mother.

*…?!*

Yes, she's here, chanting vigorously, like a devout follower. Has she always been here? Not sure, but her wardrobe is as pompous as before; maybe even a bit more, if that's even possible. Her fitted, red dress hugs her hornet-thin waist like shrink-wrap; her summer hat, wider than ever, sits like a halo atop her head; her cheekbones, high and mighty. *Did she get work done?*

All at once, the singing sheep finally silence. The chant was only the overture, a tune to summon a greater force. When, as if on cue, a small TV clicks on, in front of Bill.

# R³

"Reuse. Redream. Recyle," Nina's ethereal TV advertisement plays on loop. His followers are glued to the screen, speechless. They adore her. They adore Nina as if she were some sort of deity. But why?

"Reuse. Redream. Recyle. Making all of your dreams come true."

Conductor Bill waves his little magic wand, cuing in the orchestra… "Reuse. Redream. Recycle. Making all of your dreams come true," they all repeat in unison. "Reuse. Redream. Recycle. Making all of your dreams come true. Reuse. Redream. Recycle. Making all of your dreams come true."

The monotony of their voices makes my skin crawl. The intensity of the chant grows louder and louder. I feel oxygen rapidly leaving my lungs, not wanting to stay put. Beads of sweat materialize on my forehead as I feel every color of normality drain from my face, leaving only a paleness of pure nothingness.

*Not safe outside. Stay inside. Inside. Inside. Safe inside.*
*Not safe outside. Stay inside. Inside. Inside. Safe inside.*
*Not safe outside. Stay inside. Inside. Inside. Safe inside.*
*Not safe outside. Stay inside. Inside. Inside. Safe inside.*

Followers crowd around Bill, praising him, the air around him suddenly becoming holy. Rose, my mother, kisses his hand and looks up; her eyes glimmer eerily, moist with devotion, like they're either too alive or too dead.

I remain safely away from the crowd, as away as an RV permits, hiding behind a spider web of Christmas lights, receding from the fervor.

Bill's room is behind me. The little nook of six-by-nine calls my name. *I'm empty; you'll be safe here.*

But the voice lied to me. It wasn't empty. It was full, completely full of emptiness. Like a mighty black hole, there it sat, surrounded by stinking candles, the metallic sphere-shit-*thing-ee*, pulling everything and everyone towards it, dragging them into a whirlpool with unforgiving undertow.

Unable to help myself, I gently press my hand on it.

When in a flash,

Nina is trapped.

Nina is trapped inside a glass capsule, curled into a ball, naked, defenseless.

It shows me.

It tells me.

She's dying.

## WHAT HAD HAPPENED TO THE TIME?

*December 10, 1591?*

*The journey back has taken longer than expected. I am quite certain I've been traveling at a constant pace. If I've been mathematically precise, I should have arrived to the village by now. I've considered the possibility of having taken a detour, but I am definitely retracing my own steps.*

# R³

*I also have managed to lose track of time. My senses have been playing tricks on me as days have begun to interweave with one another. Nowhere else to go except forward. Or so I think.*

*Late December, 1591*

*I've finally made it back to the village, but don't quite remember arriving. I must have fainted due to dehydration. I woke up inside one of their small homes with a violent pounding in my head. My lips were parched. Soon after, a young woman brought me something to drink and a warm meal. I slept for another two days.*

*As soon as I was back on my feet, I did all the preparations necessary to head back into the wilderness. After reevaluating my previous travels, I concluded I've been riding in the opposite direction. I have to return back to the lake. Traveling towards a different perimeter won't help me find another town. The land here is different; this was not the same land surrounding the lake I had fallen into. That is a fact. I have to go through the lake once more.*

*As generous as before, the villagers provided me with food, supplies, and water—a larger amount*

# R³

than last time. I refused such generosity, but they insisted, eager to help. I offered my services; I could help with any repairs that needed to be done prior to my departure, anything to help repay their kindness. They asked where my travels would take me. Once I revealed I was planning to return to the lake, their faces grew pale with worry. They knew which lake I was referring to, and explained the mechanics behind the large bubble.

According to the villagers, the travelers (meaning 'us') swap places with the bubble through the lake. The traveler's body mass replaces the bubble's body mass on _this_ side, and the same occurs on the _other_ side—_my_ side. Once things take their course—meaning, once the traveler expires—, a new bubble appears and the process repeats itself. They can't tell me what causes this, or when it started, as the lake has been there since before the beginning.

There's no return, they warn me, assuring the road back would not lead me to where I wanted to go. That place is no longer there. That world is no longer there, they say. This would be a new journey, as the lake tends to _move_.

Travelers come out, they tell me, but they never go back in. They made it sound like a one-way passage, but to me it was only a lake: a pool of water. Even one-way doors can be accessed one way or the other.

They tried to persuade me to stay, but I had already made up my mind; I am returning to the lake, even if my journey is more arduous. Convinced by my determination, they finally asked for a small favor, which I immediately agreed upon. I am to take a traveler with me, the stable boy I previously met— the _magic_ boy who managed to calm my horse with natural ease. They said he was the child of destruction, born out of dead stars and fiery pits. According to them, the wondering boy appeared in the village one day, and they took him in. He had helped with the land throughout the years, but he didn't belong and his return was overdue. He had to go back to the lake. They told me his name, and made it very clear that if any harm came his way, an all-destructive force would be unleashed. I had no time to question their reasoning, as the boy approached.

He had aged, grown tall and wiry. His eyes glimmered with intricate colors and shifting patterns, like the turning wheels of a clock. I had never seen such eyes before. What struck me the most was his sudden aging; ten to fifteen years since my last visit. Inexplicably. Yet I was presumptuous, as he was not the only one. Everyone had aged

# R³

*significantly. I had failed to notice a difference among the adult villagers, but in fact, after a second revision, they were all significantly older. What had happened to the time?*

The industrial chimneys cut through the moonless sky like an elephant graveyard in the wilderness. The luscious smoke scrapes through the darkness, eventually dissolving into nothing.

Down one, two, three, four floors in the elevator, young Bill moves fast, as every security camera is on him. Every move is executed with uttermost care. He knows he shouldn't be there. He had waited until the sun went down. Until everyone had left. Until everyone was gone…

Young Bill pushes a gurney through the empty, windowless corridor. In and out of darkness, only green security lights guide his way through.

He reaches the simple white door next to the RESTRICTED AREA sign. He retrieves the silver card from his pocket, swiftly unlocks the door, and slips in rapidly. He has to act fast—he's only got a few minutes.

His footsteps echo coldly in the dark void, the large spherical vault getting closer with every step. He swipes the card a second time and enters the white room.

# R³

He pauses. He can't move, his muscles are not responding. Something isn't right. The room feels bigger. But that's not possible. *Maybe I've entered a different room?* Bill ponders. No, not possible either. Bill quickly realizes it's not the room that has changed—but its contents.

The large capsule is missing. In its place sits a glistening metallic sphere the size of a basketball. A serial code engraved on it: *001*, next to a serial number wrapped around its circumference. Bill takes a closer look. *3.14159265359.... it's Pi, just like this vault*, he thinks, *but why? And where did the incubator go?*

Incredibly confused, young Bill releases irate grunts and approaches the object, his face distorted in frustration. His hands voluntarily smack his head, punishing him for his failure.

His face suddenly breaks into a geometric outline, shifting into various flickering squares, its pieces readjusting, pixelating rhythmically, morphing into John's face.

It's me, dressed like Bill.

*Where am I? What am I doing here?*

I compose myself and open the metallic sphere, which releases a soft "hiss". Thick vapor trails slither out. I swat it away with my hands, attempting to get a clear view as I peer inside.

## R³

The sphere seems to be some sort of cooling device with a white light projecting from within, splitting the darkness in half.

Inside, three glass jars, neatly placed side by side. I remove one of the cylindrical jars. They're nearly ten inches in length and three inches wide, easily fitting on the palm of my hand. The liquid inside is yellow and has a faint glow.

There's something else inside. Squinting, I bring it up to my face and try to get a better look of the small chunks floating within. And that's when I know. I'm looking at Nina.

I close my eyes.

Blink.

Bill opens them.


There is no time.

Like a storm, Bill tears through his apartment, stuffing a small bag with cash, basic essentials, an old shoebox, any non-perishable goods, and a few shirts—not for wardrobe's sake, but to cushion the metallic sphere sitting in the middle—and nothing else. It is heavy, very heavy. It has suddenly become his cross, his burdening secret—a dreaming fugitive on the run.

*I can see him.*

*I can see Bill.*

## *Can you bring back Mr. Normal?*

Loud silence surrounds Dr. Hammond, as he sits upright on a couch, completely motionless, eyes wide open, locked in on the void. Frozen. Unblinking. Sleeping.

*I can see him.*

An alarm goes off. His body slowly reanimates, accidentally knocking an open paperback off his lap. His dilated eyes shoot to the back of his head, allowing his eyelids to fully close in a relaxed manner. His blinking goes

# R³

back to normal as he yawns and stretches his arms upward. He turns the alarm off.

It's 7:01 PM.

Mechanically, he walks through the darkness towards a table obscured by a layer of sprawled books. He immediately notices the *MONADOLOGY* book sitting wide open—out of place. A page dances erratically, pushed by a nearby air-vent.

As soon as he picks up the book, he spots the old manuscript inside. Having never seen it before, he examines it closely, flipping through its fragile pages.

Most look like diary entries, with a few rough diagrams. What catches Dr. Hammond's attention is the last page—the last diary entry—, which only contains the letter *d* at the very top, like the beginning of an unfinished word. Curious, he flips to the previous page, and reads the last few sentences: *The answer to everything, to every single question. The secret to all life and the universe. We are...*

"We are all born to..."

He flips the page: *d?*

As if suddenly remembering my somber words, Dr. Hammond reads aloud. "We are all born to ... *die*?"

All my furniture—meaning a dinning table, three chairs, and a stool—is propped up against the front door in an attempt to keep everything and everyone out, or perhaps to keep me inside. Either that or my living room has become an open space for safety. The white tiles are cold, but not too cold, the perfect, soothing amount of cold. My knees curl up into fetal position as I stare at my glowing fingertips—residuals from the electrically charged fork and lightning bolts shooting through my fingers.

*My head is empty with shapeless images.*

My head itches. I scratch it, and I scratch it hard. The pain feels good, almost orgasmic, simultaneously mitigating the itch.

Fresh blood drips off my twiggy fingers. When did they get so rawboned?

I swing a flashlight over my head, hunting for the bloody itch in the mirror. It flickers off, so I constantly have to jolt the batteries inside.

There it is. A spot directly at the top of my head, covered with dry blood and a halo of irritated skin.

This can't be good.

I push my short hair out of the way in an attempt to get a better look, but it's useless. Like anything obstructing the truth, it had to be removed.

A razor quickly does the trick. I wipe the loose hair and shaving cream off with a towel, doing my best to survive without water. I finally reveal a gash about three inches long atop of a conveniently placed, bulging lump. I stick

# R³

my skeletal finger into it. It squishes in, gruesomely causing a yellowish, viscous fluid to ooze out. It hurts like a bitch.

*Mental note: don't do that again.*

I wipe again, toweling off the residual dry blood and yucky ooze. I somehow manage to make a mess on my head, mashing together the dry shaving cream and loose sticky hairs. I can't win. Blood dribbles out again.

A soft knock at the door brings me to a halt. Have they been knocking for a while? Isaac stands against the wall, eyeballs bulging out, following my every move.

*Are you expecting someone?* I ask him.

It takes a few seconds to move the barricade of furniture off my door... I open the door a crack, wide enough to display the ridiculous towel turban currently sitting on my head.

"What?" I growl.

An average looking man with a studious but friendly face looks into my bloodshot eyes. He looks like a teacher, or perhaps a scientist of some sort. His demeanor softens, allowing pity to take over the expression in his deep wrinkles, milestones, seventy years or so of living, as he nervously readjusts his blue bowtie.

*Harmless*, I think. I let him in. *Stupid.*

I pull up a chair and drop, observing him closely. He looks around, surely having second thoughts, yet he decides to stay and sits on the chair opposite mine. I leave the flashlight on the floor facing up, beaming like a lighthouse calling out ships lost at sea. Call it mood lighting.

"Well?" I ask, while coughing up blood. Hmm, that's new.

"I'm here to help you."

"You freak-ee religious-man?"

"No. You seem to be falling apart, isn't that so?"

I take a second to chew on this. It doesn't take a rocket scientist to notice.

"My name is Dr. Walker. I want to help you," he continues, "put a lid on this... *thing* you started."

"Yapping trap-tap, you saying?" in my defense, all of these *words* sounded perfectly coherent in my head before they casually slipped out between my ensanguined lips.

"Your physical body will soon not belong to this world. We can protect you. We can make sure no harm comes to you."

Who's *we*?

"Can you bring back Mr. Normal?" I ask.

Dr. Walker wipes the spotless lens of his round glasses as he lets out a soft sigh. Must be a thing he does.

"There is no 'normal', Mr. Hammond," he begins. "*This*—is the new normal. The world in your memories no longer exists. However, only you possess the ability to stop it from spiraling out of control. You can shift it back on track."

# R³

What's he talking about? Why me? Why is it always me?

"Who izzz you-sa?"

"I'm but another spinning wheel, behind a powerful organization."

"You made the dreamer juicy-juice?"

"After the incident there was a vacuum. Dreaming was gone. Not-dreaming is a sign of a reality in decline. Our reality as we knew it had changed, yet we weren't equipped to notice the long-term differences. My wife, Cassandra, was one of the first to identify the new patterns, but even her sophisticated brain was not strong enough to endure such a void... it drove her irrevocably mad. Lost her forever to the streets. The world was entrapped in shadow; that was until Nina... Nina was different. She appeared to suddenly fill that void. We tried creating imprints out of her dreams, but their life spans were short of a few seconds once separated from her cerebral spine fluid and the other chemicals produced by her brain. That's why we synthesized R³. That's why it only works in liquid form. It's not enough to input it into your brain. Your body must absorb her in order for it to work. You have to be in communion with her. However, she wasn't enough. The well ran dry and she turned into something along the lines of a black hole. She was stolen from us. Now our existence is way off balance. Balance must be restored, Mr. Hammond. We've been watching you for a while."

# R³

"Maybe dreamersssss not need any longer—maybe the dreamers izz what we become. We be the *dreamsesss*."

"Mr. Hammond, you have no idea of the extent of the repercussions your actions have created," the doctor's voice cracked in fear. "This is beyond Pandora's Box. You've unleashed a monstrosity."

"By popping the dream-ee juice?"

"By procreating with Nina."

*What...?*

"She's an anomaly. We are the white cells fighting back, trying to survive. No one is safe. Your loved ones are in danger."

"But—you're help, you say?"

"We can offer personal safety. No harm will come to you, if you come with us."

"Others?"

"We cannot guarantee their outcome. There are powers at play that neither you nor I can command."

*Grumble, grumble.* "You speakersssss in abstractions, Mr. Help. Smoke screens and riddling threats. What does Mr. Help says it wants we forrrr?"

"*We?*" he pauses. "We need you to terminate Nina."

I laugh. At least I think it's a laugh, yet it sounds more like a squealing pig on its way to a slaughterhouse. The old man recoils, second-guessing his every decision.

"Not possible, Mr. Help," I mumble.

# R³

"Very much possible. She's both a door and a whirlpool, sucking everyone at the edge towards the center. We lost her once. This is unprecedented. You are the only bridge connecting us to her. You are the key. You need to stop this while you're still part of this world, only then will this mess begin to unwind. We are running out of time!"

"Nina is no more!" I spit out in an unexpected outburst of frustration.

"That's not entirely true. There's nothing left of her but her dreams," he begins, "however, she will come to you, and only you. It is imperative that you do this, Mr. Hammond. We will protect you. You will be safe."

"Just we-sses?"

"Just you."

*We-sses, me-sses is not enough.*

*Mother? Bill? Dr. Hammond? Everyone.*

*Me-sses is not enough.*

I get up and away from the man.

"Leave me-sses."

"Dreaming comes with a price," he stammers, not taking 'no' for an answer. "Your journey will bring you a lot of pain if you don't cooperate. You will endure intense physical... and emotional pain. The pain of feeling lost— alone in the world."

"Leave," I whisper amidst a cacophony of sanguinary coughs.

# R³

"John, you are making a terrible mistake!" yells Dr. Walker, springing up from his chair, trying to reach me. "Things have to go back into order…" but his yelling and reaching stops.

His skin is boiling red. His white eyeballs are squeezing out of their sockets. A force around him is suddenly holding him still. The old man stands, immobilized midair, chocking violently, suffocated by an invisible grip.

I don't have to move. I can feel the particles vibrating around me. The strings of creation hastily unraveling at the seams, the design collapsing like a house of cards. Oxygen slips in and out of his throat, the old man inhaling but a sliver of a drop. His color changes, red dissolving into purple. Tiny veins crown his gouging eyeballs distorting his face completely. His body rises… the tip of his feet barely touching the ground.

He is going to die.

I know he is going to die.

He knows he is going to die.

"Ple—ease…" the sound wheezes out, barely intelligible.

This man will die.

But not today.

The old man drops on all fours, gasping loudly for air. Oxygen, a simple element, speedily pours into his lungs once again, quenching his thirst for the world of the living.

# R³

His face goes back to its normal color. His eyes decompress and fit back into their sockets.

More terrified than satisfied, he jumps to his feet and scurries, crushing his glasses on his way out.

Drawn to the second most interesting thing, I look at my fingers. One of my nails has turned slightly purple. It's quite a beautiful discoloration.

I snap it off with ease.

It barely bleeds. Yellow liquid oozes out of it.

Am I slowly rotting?

*Falling apart,* Mr. Help said.

Fall-eeeen—aaapppppp—


—tart.

## *A universal joke.*

*Wrapping, wrappy, wrappity-wrap, around my knocker, around my finger.*

I pace back and forth, looking for something, or not looking, but only pacing, as there's nothing there to look for.

*Can't leave. Must leave. Not safe outside. Safe Inside. Safe inside. Can't leave. Must leave. Can't leave. Must leave. Can't leave. Must leave.*

# R³

The dead man hovers behind me, pulling me back, reeling me in. But the dead man doesn't know better, he's dead.

*Yes...*

*...John knows...*

*...outside will consume me-sses.*

*Must leave.*

I fall in and out of light, dragging my left foot, pushing myself up with a crutch down the concrete sidewalk. My heavy breathing, practically wheezing, stings like shards of glass slipping into every crevice between my ribs.

The towels wrapped around my head feel heavy, but it's the cloudy darkness creeping into my eyes that has me worried. Like farm oxen plowing the fields, I can push through until my spine snaps, but without my sight, I feel lost.

I'm running out of time, steadily falling into a pit of darkness. I can feel my eyes fading, turning into rusty pearls. I don't want to go blind.

The homeless woman sees me limp from down the street, her eyes following me with caution. Awake. Alert.

"We are perpetual living mirrors of the universe," she says. *Cassandra...*

This time, she doesn't laugh.

The joke is over.

# R³

There's an unusual stillness that screams to remain undisturbed. The grandfather clock tics away deeper than ever, like a heartbeat underscoring a Hitchcock movie, guiding your hero into a bottomless pit. My mother's living room has become a cavernous lair for shadows, kept at bay only by flickering candles and a blazing fireplace, crackling furiously. It's the epicenter of this new world, like a burning sun, facing my mother who is as poised as a statue.

"Mother-er?"

"Oh, sweet bug! Is it you?" she turns, revealing her mud-mask covered face. It's nerve-wracking. She wears a crimson silk robe and a cucumber slice on each eye; yet, she can feel my presence, following my every move with her vegetable goggles.

"I've missed you terribly! Sit. Let me look at you."

I limp over, weary, taking a seat next to her on the couch. She, however, does not remove her cucumber spectacles, but still finds a way to *see*. This feels like a cruel joke based on my increasing blindness.

"I have a romantic rendezvous with a very fine gentleman tonight," she says placing her perfectly manicured hand on my knee. "The nanny will be here shortly."

"Danger is here. Cometh with me-sser, keep you safe," I try to sputter out sentences, but incomplete words take their place, so I tug at her arm in an attempt to get her immediate attention.

# R³

"I'm not going anywhere!" she shrieks snatching her arm away. "Don't be ridiculous. Didn't you hear? I have to get ready for my date."

"I must stay with you, mother-er."

"Nonsense! I'll give you some cough syrup and you'll sleep like you're dead. A sweet, dream-less, sleep."

"Falling apart, everything. No time. Running!" I beg. "The red juice trickling. Look at me!"

She does, but doesn't—only her cucumber eyes. "You look fine! Stop being so self-centered. It's my night. I have a date with a doctor. I have to look good for the doctor. He's a doctor, you know?" She goes off on a looping tangent. "I have to look good for the doctor. He's such a dream!"

There's nothing I can do, not with this strength—or lack thereof—, not while holding myself up with a crutch. The possibility of other exit routes seem to fade away as she swims in the interiors of her subconscious—the new reality, the new world, kicking from the inside like an unborn child, dying to come out.

As I limp towards the front door, I take one last look at the fading shell of what my mother used to be. Responding to my mental longing, she turns, but she's not her anymore. Nina has taken her place.

I slip in a panic when I try to race over, landing on my back with a dry and chilling crack. Air wheezes out of my lungs as I roll on the floor in excruciating pain. Every last inch of me has shattered. It even sounded like I shattered.

Glass. Crystals.

But it wasn't me that crashed. My crutch had shot out from under me and into the wall, producing shattered edges around a beaming hole—as if a rock had been thrown through a window, except this was supposed to be solid concrete. The edges of this glass-like wall glow, creating flickering shards, fireflies flashing like broken pixels. Light beams out as I peek inside, blocking the intense whiteness with my hand, my pupils dilating in a frenzy, unable to focus.

Holding my back in pain, I look up, my eyes searching for Nina, but as expected she's long gone; the back of my mother's head remains... a ticking bomb.

I manage to crawl into the shattered exit, leaving my mother and this world behind.

Sandy snow wraps around my feet. The horizon extends into nothing, leading to more nothing towards nothing. I've never seen such a clean field, free from any obstructions, free from any imperfections.

A layer of crystalline snow mist sits dusted atop my turban hat. It trickles down my neck, icy, melting against my relatively warm body. Yet I don't feel cold. I can't decide if it's a magical quality of the place, or if my body has fallen into a state of perpetual numbness. I remove my shoes, suddenly feeling the urge to sink my toes into the plush snow; so frosted, so immaculate, no trace of impurities—no dirt, no mud. My feet on the other hand, are disgustingly imperfect. My toenails have grown into black and blue claws, and my feet have a general overtone of yellow. I bury them under the snow.

Hiding them.

Better.

The world behind me is not the same. Protruding from under the snow, crystal shards grow upright, resembling glass cacti. I wrap my hand around their surface; firm and clean. An unexpected level of warmth seeps through my fingertips.

That's when I see her, staring out at the blue sky, her fiery hair flying wildly among the gentle snowfall.

She smiles wholeheartedly as I approach. Her warm, delicate hands wrap around my face, holding it lovingly, with no shred of judgment. I can feel my incredulous eyes bounce back and forth, unable to move, unable to speak.

"The end. Is it now?" I finally manage to say.

"The end isn't the end. It's the beginning."

# ROSE'S DATE

My robotic mother wraps her arm around Dr. Hammond's like a starving octopus. He lets her, captivated by the scene unfolding before his eyes.

Consumed by his own haunting obsession, Bill's eyes have developed a white layer on them, turning him partially blind. His followers hum and chant their usual, dissonant melody.

# R³

Bill wraps his spotty hands around the metallic sphere, reading the geometric frieze with his fingertips. Dr. Hammond's eyes are instantly drawn to the unusual object. He doesn't know why, but amidst the chanting frenzy, he can't stop looking at it.

*I remember seeing the contents...*

*The jars...*

*The liquid...*

*Nina.*

With a sense of recognition beyond any reasonable explanation, Dr. Hammond suddenly understands. He understands what's inside the sphere. He understands what's inside the jars. Perhaps, *understands* is not the correct word, but it's the simplest way to describe how *my* mentally stored visual perception—John's perception—had found its way, as if downloaded, into the dark corners of Dr. Hammond's own mind. We are in sync. Somehow.

I see this happening.

I feel this happening.

And I'm not even there.

"Reuse. Redream. Recycle. Making all of your dreams come true," they sing.

*Reuse. Redream. Recycle. Making all of your dreams come true,* they promise.

After the ceremony, the woman who calls herself my mother kisses Bill's semi-decomposing hand with deep appreciation.

# R³

Like an ancient underwater creature who's been sleeping for millennia, Bill opens his cavernous mouth lethargically, suddenly enlightened by some spark of wisdom. "The all-seeing One Eye will be here before we know it. It will be born and it will light our path. Its powers—limitless."

Corroded by his own gluttonous holiness, Bill's distracted murky eyes leave the metallic sphere. It sits, unsupervised, at the back of the RV, reeling Dr. Hammond in with extraordinary force.

## THE WELL RAN DRY

"They're not stocking our supplies anymore. The well ran dry," says the counter clerk in a voice burdened with annoyance.

Young Bill's hair falls onto his face, uncombed, frazzled, uncontrolled—like him.

"Are you sure? You sure you're not hoarding a box in the back? Your personal little stash??" he accuses, scrambling for the right words when none come out.

# R³

"For the last time, *sir*," the clerk says firmly, "we are out. There are no R³s available anymore. We haven't received a shipment in weeks."

Blood drains out of Bill's young face as his current reality slowly shatters.

The small TV stacked in a corner of his cramped, dirty motel room blares loudly, illuminating the otherwise somber area with its fluorescence. Styrofoam containers and take-out paper bags crowd every surface of the room—some with days old food still sitting in them and the swarm of flies that chaperon them.

A tower made out of empty R³ bottles sits on top of the only small table by the TV. A rat scampers by.

"...bringing us back to living in a dream-less world," the TV reporter says, hugging her microphone. "On related news, a sudden upsurge on the snowflakes' stock market clearly shows it's been driving more consumers to the store as a direct result of..."

Young Bill digs through every cabinet under the dwarf bathroom sink. Cleaning supplies, plunger, brush; all land on the bathroom floor, rattling, screaming at his recklessness. Finally, he stops, retrieving a small box. An old shoebox. He blows the dust off the lid and removes a small, silvery piece from inside. A gun. He looks at it intently. The features on his face fragment, splitting into tiny puzzle pieces, shifting and pixelating in no particular order, constantly changing and repositioning like a Rubik's cube until the pieces progressively reassemble, displaying John's face—my face.

*What are you doing, Bill?*

**THE YEAR OF THE NOW**

Bill enters his private corner in the RV lead by his milky eyes. The metallic sphere sits on its usual spot. He closes the curtain behind him, disconnecting from the blind followers and the outside world.

He closes his eyes, pressing his hands on the container. However, something is wrong. He frowns, presses harder, expecting something to happen, but it doesn't. He unlocks the latch and opens the lid with a "hiss". His face distorts with a mixture of terror and disbelief.

Bill takes a few steps back and collapses on the floor, his worn-out heart suffocated with anguish. A pitiful whimper slips out between his dry lips.

The metallic sphere is empty.

## *His brain has turned to mush.*

Dr. Hammond starts up the machine.

From inside a bag, he retrieves the three jars containing the yellow serum. A glowing, geometric outline suddenly bleeds through his face, allowing it to shift and rearrange itself, until it gradually pixelates into me, dressed exactly like Dr. Hammond.

# R³

With meticulous care, I pour the contents of the jars into a large glass container with a narrow mouth, connected to the iron-lung incubator. The unused hammer sits on the table.

Once the machine is fully running, I take my spot on the chaise lounge and inject the IV into my arm and cortex. I monitor the stats with a small remote control as a set of numbers blink repeatedly, going up. As soon as they stop, a green light goes on.

I hit the red button on the switch.

Nina's serum begins to pump out of the glass container. A few seconds later, a more radiant version of the serum flows out of the incubator into a tube connected to my IV.

Finally the serum reaches both my arm and cortex, causing my body to jolt violently. I clench my fists, trying as hard as I can to endure the agonizing pain that is paralyzing my entire body. My eyes flip open as a loud gasp rushes out of my mouth. My eyeballs are clouded with frosted white.

Lights flutter across my eyelids. A liquid suddenly perforates my iris, mimicking the membrane of a cell-like bubble. Images flip like a slide show through the visual innards of my brain.

An indescribable level of joy overpowers my pleasure core as Nina, on a swing, laughs hysterically, full of life. She drops onto her back, in a fit of melodic giggles, orgasmic music to my ears.

But memory lane takes a sharp turn as a doctor examines Nina's vitals. There's something wrong. Her skin is pallid, her face is gaunt. Her kaleidoscopic eyes tear up in fear as the color slowly fades out of them. A large, womb-like capsule envelops her. Droning hums reverberate inside her ears, forcing electrical stimuli into her delicate brain. Bright lights flash, rupturing her dilated pupils. She can't breathe.

My body is taken over by tremors, wanting it to stop, but the slide show continues, far from being done; it's an unstoppable force, which has something to teach. It takes us back in time...

Nina meets me in the club for the first time. I follow her.

I let the wall guide me back into my tiny living room, but the wall warns me—something is wrong. And the wall is right.

Isaac is frozen, his back turned and his eyes glued to the coffee table in the middle of the room. The R³ bottle, the pharmaceutical bottles, an old syringe—the buffet of drugs all spread over. On perfect display. On a silver platter.

It's over. From behind, Isaac slowly reaches towards his waistcoat—a gun? Cold sweat trickles down my neck and down my spine. It has to be a gun.

# R³

Isaac turns briskly, his hand wrapped around a black object, but the hammer finds its way into my shaky hand before he fully faces me. Lovingly hugged between my fingers, the hammer swings hastily, cutting through the air, finally landing on Isaac's fragile skull.

Blink. I'm gone.

Blink. Dr. Hammond's hand is now hugging the hammer impacted into Isaac's skull.

Crack.

Isaac collapses.

Blink. A confused Dr. Hammond now stands outside of my apartment, still holding the bloody hammer. Somehow I'm seeing all of this—from above, from below.

*He was there...*

Blood speckles his face and shirt.

*He killed Isaac. I wasn't there. Yet I was there... as him. He was me. But who am I, if not me?*

"John, do not open the door. You hear me? Do not open the door." Nina warns me, before hanging up.

*She knew...* She was protecting me, stopping me from facing myself, stopping my worlds from coming undone.

Disoriented, Dr. Hammond turns and knocks twice on my door, gently. Then, his cell phone goes off. The jingle.

# R³

I'm inside my apartment; I can hear the jingle, just like before. I know Dr. Hammond is outside looking down the hallway, hoping to remain unseen; I know he's there. I can feel him... an extension of myself.

In the midst of a panic attack, Dr. Hammond flees, exiting the apartment building, allowing his phone to ring until it fades completely, leaving behind only the sound of my echoing heartbeat. I close my eyes. The serum takes me somewhere else...


*Where am I?*

Nina lays on a gurney, wearing a white gown. Her body blends in with the blasting white lights. She is very much pregnant. Her face appears emotionless, dead, coated with sweat, the surrounding hair dampened with excessive moisture.

"Our son will be born to—" Her voice cracks.

She screams in pain. She's giving birth.

"The cord is wrapped around his neck!" one doctor yells, "You must stop fighting! You're killing him!"

*My sweet... sweet... Johnny. Our Johnny.*


I descend past sewage pipes and electrical wiring, through concrete and wood, flowing like a ghost, until I arrive at a dark and gritty hospital room; a German expressionistic sanitary nightmare, with sharp corners and devouring shadows. I hover, suspended midair over two

# R³

doctors wearing scrubs and breathing masks. They look over a brain scan.

"His brain has turned to mush," the first one sings. "Don't you agree, doctor?"

"Yes, doctor. Indeed," the second one adds.

"He needs a new one," the first one sings. "Don't you agree, doctor?"

"Yes, doctor. Indeed," the second one adds.

I float through the wall, into the adjacent room with mold pushing through the tiles. Strapped on an operation chair, under a hot fluorescent spotlight, Dr. Hammond's limp body sinks, respectfully abiding to the laws of gravity.

Disheveled, he half-opens his eyes, studying his environment. He tries to move, but his hands are restrained against the chair. Wires and hooks are attached to his eyes, head and mouth, immobilizing his jaw. Viscous drool drips onto his lap. He notices the dotted pattern on the hospital gown. His legs are bare, hardly covered by the medical fabric.

Fear crawls like fire ants all over his body. He squirms violently trying to release himself, but the straps won't budge. Hands, arms, chest, feet—all firmly secured against the metallic chair, which in turn is bolted into the moldy floor. His eyes follow a thick, black chord growing from behind the chair, trailing into a large machine that looks like a generator. A small screen frames a dial needle, which increases with every passing second. 10. 50. 80. 100. 150. 200. Volts. Then it stops.

A stream of white fluid cuts through Dr. Hammond's body, jolting him in his seat and numbing his senses. The dial needle goes back to zero. As his head hangs, more drool drips onto his lap. His eyes float inside their sockets, trying to further examine the room hidden in the shadows. A cabinet holds medical supplies such as needles and a collection of jars securing fluids and organs—HAZARDOUS and TOXIC symbols on every single one of them. A small sink drips loudly, not fully tightened.

Stiletto heels staccato snappily down then hall. He sees a silhouette approaching through the rectangular windows on the double doors. Someone is coming. Someone to help? Someone to set him free?

The doors swing open, making way for a petite woman in a fitted, red tailored dress and wide-brimmed hat. Dr. Hammond squints hard, hoping to identify friend or foe. She stops abruptly at the sight of him, letting out a faint gasp. Shadows mask her face, but her voice is unmistakable. *This can't be real*, he thinks…

"Sweet bug… what have they done to you?" Rose whines, finally looking up, revealing her face—fully covered with bandages, except for a small sliver exposing her overly done lips. Dr. Hammond instantly recoils, the wiring on his jaw allowing only faint whimpers to slip through.

# R³

"My poor, poor baby... Thank you so much for doing this, you have no idea what this means to me," she baby talks as she removes the bandages on her face, each one peeling off slowly, stretching icky residuals oozing from her rotting, disfigured face. "Mommy loves you, mommy loves you dearly. Thank you for giving me your skin. I need it. I need it badly. Mommy needs to be young again."

*Mommy?*

A chunk of meat falls off. Her skin is practically melting off her bones, dripping like thick pudding.

Dr. Hammond panics, wailing and shaking his arms violently, trying to free himself. The needle dial goes up again and an electric shock blasts through his fragile body. His eyes force themselves open; his eyelids seem to weight a ton.

Suddenly, the dark hallway from which Rose entered extends to surreal depths like an accordion; its walls fly off swiftly, revealing the geometric 'space' adorned by pixel-fireflies and crawling light beams.

The room boxing them shakes. Its foundation no longer rooted on a secure surface, they fall victim to evaporating gravity. Dr. Hammond's eyes are about to dart out of their sockets as his movements become explosively violent.

A crackling sound shatters all noise, leaving everything to his ears forever muted.

# R³

"Here you go, sweet-bug. It's time to dream," says Rose, as she feeds the memory of my young self some R³ out of a magical blue bottle…

Dr. Hammond throws up violently into the toilet. He is at home, his tie loosened, the top buttons of his shirt undone. Did he dream that? *Or did I dream that?* Black gunk forcibly pours out of his mouth, making his eyes bloodshot, and his face flushed, from the never-ending expulsion of the strange substance taking over his body. His eyes are hypersensitive to light and his ears to sound.

Nina runs into the bathroom and abruptly stops at the sight of him. Dr. Hammond squints, *is this real?*

Nina panics. "Johnny? What's wrong??"

*Johnny?*

Flustered, she places her hand on his back but immediately recoils, as Dr. Hammond bends over vomiting more violently. Nina presses her back against the cold wall, trapped, tears streaming down her flawless complexion.

The room around Dr. Hammond spins.

He collapses, the last bit of oxygen wheezing out of his now empty lungs.

## *The Crystal Field.*

Darkness consumes my tiny apartment, save for an invasive flashlight and a candle here and there. My furniture is piled on one side of the room, blocking the door, leaving the entire floor exposed.

I sit in the middle of the room, scratching my forever-itching head. I can sense darkness wrapping over my bleak eyes.

# R³

I dreamt last night. A dream with my eyes open, a dream with my eyes closed—what difference does it make?

And so my dream begins…

Two men journeyed through a thick forest with trees as tall as the eye could register. Branches acted as restricting gates allowing but faint beams of light to pass through. The men rode on horses, but their pace was steady, as foliage grew thicker and thicker, making it almost impossible for them to continue. The older, seemingly more experienced man took the lead. A younger man followed, silent; his apprehensive eyes glued to the ground, every speck of color hidden within them, like Nina's. Their faces were thin, and their clothes, dirty. The young man was weak and never got off his horse. The leader had made a promise, a promise to someone important, to protect this young man, as he was of value. He was not to let anything *bad* happen to him, but he hadn't expected disease.

Their journey took them into rocky mountains, across a desert. The horses were weak and thirsty. The leader fed the young man berries from inside a leather pouch. Their water supply was running low.

Halfway through the mountain range, one of the horses collapsed, dying from exhaustion or sunstroke.

# R³

Unwilling to share the fate of the horse, they set camp for the night and cooked part of its meat, hoping to fuel themselves, at least until their next encounter with supplies, which could be soon, late, or never.

This man was looking for something. He was looking for a lake, a pool of water, which they should've come across by now. Yet he was told it had moved, and indeed it had. However, his perseverance remained unchanged—he couldn't go back now, even though *back* was where he wanted to be.

By the time they arrived to a vast, snowy plain, the second horse was gone. Beards covered their faces—frozen icicles hung from them, frosty jewelry. They found themselves surrounded by emptiness. White and more white. The older man's eyes showed panic and confusion. The young man was getting weaker, barely holding his weight with the aid of a makeshift walking stick.

A few miles in, the plain had suddenly changed and was no longer flat; crystal spikes protruded from the icy ground. The man recognized this place. He saw it in a dream. *It's a sign*, he thought, *we are here*. With renewed energy and hope, he cut through the crystal field, finally coming to a stop.

Before him, a wide opening, at least thirty feet in diameter, sat free of crystal spikes. In its place, hundreds of frozen animals—horses, tigers, lions, elephants, deer—

protruded from the ground. Thin coats of shimmering ice blanketed their lifeless bodies, capturing forever in time their attempt to break free, to escape, to swim out… it was a graveyard of ice. And that's when he knew his search was over. He had finally arrived to the lake.

He wanted to explain to the young man that they had to get to the other side, that they had to go *inside* the lake, but his excitement got the best of him. Expecting to find trapped water below the icy crust, he retrieved a rifle from inside his bag, and began smashing the butt end against the permafrost. After a few hard hits, he looked down—not even a scratch. Desperation took over as his tired eyes scanned the area for something—anything—he could use to break through. White clouds puffed out the young man's mouth as he rested against a large ice crystal, too tired to take another step.

The leader swung his rifle and, cutting through the air, smashed it into one of the crystal spikes, snapping a sharp "arm" off. He picked up the pronged ice shard, wrapping his arms around it. It was heavy.

Releasing a primal growl, he lifted the object above his head, using every ounce of strength left in him, and speared the crystal into the ice, producing a mild crack. He approached the point of impact, finding a deep dent marking the spot. Thin cracks fanned out elegantly like veins in the thick ice.

# R³

Excited by the result, he retrieved the crystal and once again, gathered all his strength to raise it above his head. Every blood vessel in his body burst as his face boiled red with untamable anger. Anger towards this new governless world. Anger at the irrefutable lack of logic he had come to face. Anger at being abandoned by his lucidity and bearings, which all his life had held both his feet secured to the ground, to his reality. When his back let out a dry *snap*, causing him to release the heavy crystal mid-lift.

The leader recoiled in agony, tears freezing around his eyes. He reached out for his backside, hoping to minimize the pain, but he could barely move, prisoner to his decaying mechanics.

Feeling defeated, he rolled to his side. The crystal spike had shattered, chunks the size of his fist scattered around him. Hope was becoming a fading concept, withering, along with everything else in his life. Until he saw it. Hiding between the crystalized wildlife, a dark fissure painted on the ice. The unexpected darkness hidden in the depths became his ray of hope.

The leader crawled towards the cavity—it was about a few feet wide and several feet long. He pressed his face inside, but was unable to see anything; only absolute, dense unperturbed darkness. He peered over at the young man, who slept undisturbed. Or at least he hoped he slept. The leader grabbed one of the crystal rocks and dropped it inside. It bounced off a dry surface, echoing loudly. *Perhaps five to seven feet deep, but no water?* he thought.

Curious, he crawled inside, down the rabbit hole, the mouth just wide enough for him to squeeze past, allowing himself to be swallowed whole.

The interior was cavernous and uneven. Filtered sunlight beamed through thin patches of ice above him, illuminating areas of the narrow passage. Feet first, he crouched and slid down the sole opening, a low tunnel, watching his head for stalagmites of ice. The shaft ended abruptly, leaving him hanging off a shallow ledge. His feet easily touched the ground below, allowing him to drop with confidence. Wary, he turned around, looked down and stopped. A pit; so deep and so wide, it could hide a skyscraper inside. And stairs. Dozens upon dozens of narrow and slightly uneven pieces of rock jutting out of the smooth wall cascaded into a spiral.

The leader faltered. Terror immobilized his every muscle. *What is this place?* Tremors took over his body as he descended—his breath hanging, growing icier and icier.

Thirty. Thirty-one. Thirty-two… he counted every step, the walls growing wider and wider with every circular loop. Three-hundred-and-fourteen steps later, he reached the firm bottom. He found himself suddenly surrounded by barren walls, save for a hole in the ground in the shape of a perfectly proportional square. It was wide enough for him

# R³

to squeeze through. Knowing he was about to go out of light's faint, protective reach, he took a deep breath and continued down the orifice.

After a few seconds of attempting to readjust to the darkness, his dry eyes squinted, straining to focus. He was inside a perfect cube. He counted his steps, rubbing his hand against the smooth, cold wall and ceiling, hanging just above his head. The missing presence of ice surprised him. Whatever material was used to create such a room was heavy, and unyielding. Yet perfect smoothness had been attained through impressive craftsmanship.

Walls, ceiling and floor, however, didn't touch. A thin crevice, just wide enough to allow him to squeeze his fingers inside, held all six pieces apart. *If they are not touching, what is holding the walls in place?* Gusts of wind squealed in and out of the crevices with unnerving frequency and precision. The constant rhythm resembled that of a ticking clock, or even a heartbeat. *Where is all this high-pressured air coming from?* he pondered, but even that became a secondary concern once he discovered the cardinal object in the room.

A cube sat like an altar at the exact center of the chamber. The wind gusted around it, maintaining its steady rhythm. He kneeled and tried to move the cube, but it wouldn't budge. Intricately carved lines adorned the surface, presumably nothing more than geometric patterns. His hands made their way over the entire surface, reading it like Braille, examining the patterns in the dark. He could tell the grooves in the rock were made with extreme care and precision. Not a single scrape or chip out of place. Every line, every pattern, flowed smoothly into the other.

That's when he noticed the silence. Ear-splitting silence. The winds had stopped. Unnerved, his heart pounded audibly, almost too loudly, alerting the world of his panic. Far above, somewhere on the safer surface, he could hear the young man coughing violently. Without warning, the winds returned, roaring through the crevices in a tempestuous outpour, propelling him against the walls with tornado-like strength.

Short of breath, the leader exited the chamber and made his way back, sprinting up two steps at a time. He clawed his way out through the fissure, digging his nails into ice and rock, pulling himself out, not stopping until he was a good ten—safe—feet away from the opening.

And then I woke up. I think.

I remove the hat and bloody bandages and discard them unceremoniously. Dry blood encrusts my scalp. I can feel it; a slit on my head emanates a faint glow in the darkness of the room. I see myself, floating, examining myself from

# $R^3$

above, staring at the *thing* growing out of my head… a tiny, nebulous, semi-opaque membrane. The itching has stopped.

"*We are now connected. We are now one. Wake up, John. You know what you have to do,*" I hear Nina's voice inside my brain.

Somewhere inside.

Deep inside.

Air pushes out of my lungs in the form of a dry gasp. Suddenly a beam of white light pours out from both my eyes and mouth. Objects around the room begin to levitate. The wooden floor begins to ripple, as if it had suddenly liquefied—projecting outwards, holding me at the center.

## *Everything falls in this reality.*

Bill weeps in a corner lamenting the loss of his holy glass jars. He digs out a gun from inside a drawer and accommodates the muzzle inside his mouth. Holding back tears, he squeezes the trigger tightly, about to make the decisive pull.

# R³

When a thought interrupts him. A thought he can't make sense of. Something disguised as a memory. He sees himself; his younger self, in a rundown motel, brandishing the same gun. His younger self opens the metallic sphere containing the glass jars and holds one up, admiring the beauty of the light filtering through the yellow serum. This triggers another memory, transporting him to a different place and time; to the yellow serum exiting the glass container into the iron-lung incubator, into Dr. Hammond's arm, inside his garage.

A sudden sense of recognition takes over Bill. A vision. His connection with the serum suddenly revealed to him its current location, as if communicating a message. It's talking to him.

Bill slowly lowers the gun.

The vacuum.

Light-flares have increased in frequency, radiating colorful, geometric pixelations, all on a black canvas. A constant fluidity of rapidly shifting perspective, waves in and out, interlocking with each other, fading into sand-like dust, faster and faster.

The shiny, metallic object moves swifter than ever, cutting through the amalgamation of color in the space-like environment.

# R³

Dr. Hammond's house is suffocated by darkness. Street light filters through partially open blinds, painting streaks onto the wooden floorboards. The door creaks open.

Bill holds his gun still, the handle warm from sitting in his hand, and moves through the shadows on full alert. He makes way down the hallway and kicks open the door connecting to the garage, aiming with a steady hand. His anger is instantly replaced by terror.

Dr. Hammond lays on the chaise lounge connected to the IV. Blood specks on his face and shirt. His hand clutches the bloody hammer. His eyes are open, but clouded. He doesn't seem to notice Bill's sudden, unwarranted presence. He's in a different world, in some kind of self-induced trance.

On the floor, next to Dr. Hammond, lays Isaac. His skull bashed in. Dead with his eyes agape. The missing body finally materialized.

*All the loose and continuously-multiplying time lines are merging into one... Dr. Hammond, Bill, mother, me...*

Bill approaches the large glass container holding Nina's serum and observes it, longingly. His eyes soften. Following the tubes exiting the container, his eyes land on the iron-lung incubator. He frowns in suspicion, *what is that?*

# R³

He approaches the large device, finally viewing its contents: John asleep. Me. Or so it appears to be.

Incredulous, Bill approaches, examining closely, resting his hands on the glass. He notices a faint glow beaming out of my head. I can sense his eyes widening as he moistens his thin lips. *The third eye.*

Bill lifts the glass open and grabs a knife off the worktable, ready to extirpate, when *her* voice interrupts.

*Wake up.*

My eyes flip open, waking up from Dr. Hammond's hypnosis experiment. Cloudiness no longer obstructs my sight, exposing my iris' clear, diamond shaped colors. Bill gasps, dropping the knife with a subtle thud.

The R³ bottle sits on the table. The TV is on; static. This is mother's home. I can smell it. Musty. Thick. Memories take over, memories of the past, memories of when I was a kid.

*You will provide me access to your subconscious*, Dr. Hammond had said, *maybe even access to secrets you've been keeping from yourself...*

Mother is passed out on the couch, clutching an empty wine bottle. I'm nowhere in sight.

A shadow creeps in through an open window, quietly crawling around the furniture, remaining hidden in the shadows. Young Bill stealthily pokes his head around the couch, observing his surroundings.

Everything is motionless.

He tip toes to the kitchen and goes through all the cabinets and the pantry. He opens one particular cabinet and halts. Smiles. Two packs of at least twelve $R^3$s each. He grabs them and stuffs them inside a black duffel bag.

*Oh, Bill...*

Happy with his find, he heads back to the front door but stops at the sight of an open $R^3$ bottle sitting on the coffee table; the one mother had been previously feeding me. His eyes sparkle with greed as he reaches out to grab it.

He can't see me coming.

The TV box cleans up the static dust until the screen is pure white. My tiny frame pushes through the framed glass, crawling out of the box and into the *other* side. Bill's side.

My mother sleeps on the couch. That's when I see young Bill, his back to me, packing the last $R^3$.

My $R^3$.

I have no fear.

I know no fear.

The floor creaks under my small feet. Feeling my eyes on him, Bill turns and jolts at the sight of me; only four, wearing fire truck pajamas. He attempts to slowly hide the gun behind his back and presses his index finger against his lips: "shh".

# R³

I calmly exit the incubator in Dr. Hammond's garage. Bill stumbles, stepping back with his gun pointed at me in trembling hands. I approach him, getting incredibly close, cornering him like a dying animal. Bill aims, scared, but can't seem to pull the trigger. Like before.

With a soothing smile, I press my index finger against my lips: "shh". That's when I begin to glow. Sounds crackle, muting everything else. Bill opens his mouth wide in terror but no sound comes out.

Only light.

Young Bill squints as he gets lost in my innocent, kaleidoscopic eyes. Drawn in by some hypnotic gravitational pull, he reaches out to touch my little-kid shoulder. His curious frown instantly inverts itself upon impact.

Uncontrollable glimmers of light and images all speed past young Bill's eyes for a tenth of a second, much like when he'd touched Nina's capsule.

His body is shoved backwards as if repelled by an electric shockwave, landing him on the floor. Freaked out, young Bill bounces back onto his feet and rushes towards the door. But just as he's slipping out, the door swings violently, crushing his arm against the frame. He lets out a piercing shriek.

Neighbors get stirred up next door. Mother doesn't even move.

Determined, he pulls, trying to free himself, feeling the R³ bottle wrapped securely between his fingers. But the door tightens, crushing his shoulder and humerus; bone splinters packed between muscles and skin. His nerve endings weaken, his blood vessels choke. His arm is slowly dying.

I push the door harder. Bill lets out a broken whimper, followed by a pitiful wail. The grip of his hand loosens. The R³ bottle begins to slip…

When a banging pain on the side of my head makes the world tilt sideways. In reality it is me who is falling; my feet leave the floor, my body lands gently atop the shaggy rug.

The door releases Bill immediately, who bolts and doesn't look back, taking my R³ with him.

My mother allows her wine bottle, her treacherous weapon, to slip out of her hand, landing softly next to me on the rug. *Everything falls in this reality, everything falls and lands*, I remember thinking, as my mother wrapped her arms around my small, limp body, muted tears streaming down her cheeks, unaware that the coloration in my eyes was languidly fading like a candle burning off the last inch of its wick.

# R³

Young Bill grabs an R³ bottle and rations it, spreading it into several small containers. He labels each one with the date, month and year, and places them inside the mini fridge provided in the motel room. He drinks one rationed serving. His body shudders with pleasure. His shapeless arm is deeply bruised. Dark purple capillaries have begun to crawl, extending towards the tip of his fingers. He can't move his hand. But he doesn't care. Not right now. He's somewhere else.

In front of him sits a pyramid of stacked R³ bottles.

A lifetime supply.

A house of cards.


Young Bill creeps into a run-down locker room with an engorged, black duffel bag in hand. He stores it inside locker "314".

Same bag.

Same locker.

He slams it shut.

## *It's time, isn't it?*

A reflection in a mirror: Nina, she touches her own face smiling.

"I'm so beautiful…"

But Nina is only a deceiving image on the reflective glass. Lost in her distortion, lost in Nina's reflection, Rose caresses her face, her skin sluggishly melting off as if it were made out of wax.

# R³

A hand extends out toward her seemingly asking permission for a dance. An orchestral version of the jingle plays on the radio. A comforting lullaby inundating her living room.

"Oh, you're such a doll," my mother mutters, teeth falling out with every word, like leaves off a tree in autumn.

She accepts my offer and slow dances with me, pressing her chin on my shoulder. The top of my head continues to emit a faint glow.

"You came back."

"I'd never let them hurt you," I say warmly.

"Oh, sweet bug," she looks up at me, her eyes moist with longing, tired of carrying the burden of guilt on her shoulders. "You were born with your eyes open on the brightest of days, the one most suffused with sun." She smiles and looks down, caught up in a thought. "It's time, isn't it?"

*Merging into one...*

I nod, smiling.

"How do I look?"

"Beautiful," I confess with unpolluted honesty.

"I'm ready, sweet bug. Momma is ready."

And then, I begin to glow.

## *John.*

The leader sits close to a crackling fire in the middle of a vast rocky plain; no snow in sight. Stars glitter brilliantly in the moonless night sky.

Opposite him, by the fire, the young man sweats and shivers under a blanket on the ground. A severe fever. He tosses and turns; releasing weak moans.

# R³

The leader nods off, hugging his rifle; large bags hang under his eyes. Unable to keep his heavy lids open, he slowly drifts into deep sleep, perhaps dreaming. Or perhaps not.

A coyote howls in the distance.

The leader's head falls forward, causing him to awaken. The fire has dimmed to an orange glow in the firewood. Amidst the surrounding darkness, his eyes catch an intruder.

Now alert, he reacts instinctively. Getting up on his feet, he aims his weapon at the mysterious figure crouched by the sick man. "Step back! I mean it!"

*Protect him with your life*, they said.

The crouched figure rises from the ground; a Native American man, withered by time, with skin like dry leather. He holds a small bowl in one hand, having fed some of the contents to the sick young man whose weak lips move, yearning for more.

"What did you give him?"

Confused, but not afraid, the Native American man looks directly into the leader's bloodshot eyes. He doesn't even blink. He takes a step forward causing the armed man to take a step back, never lowering his weapon.

"I'm warning you!"

The young man begins to move, slowly awakening, groaning. Distracted, the armed leader lowers his guard, allowing the Native American to crouch, in an attempt to return to the sick man's side.

"Don't move I said!" threatens the leader once again, raising his rifle. The intruder does so, but the leader quickly realizes it's not due to his weapon.

The intruder's attention is glued to the sick man, who slowly begins to rise, holding his head in intense pain. He groans, loudly. The pain increases. He holds his head with both hands as if it were about to explode. The leader's panic spreads.

"What did you do to him??"

The groans intensify, shattering the man's nerves.

*If any harm comes his way, an all-destructive force will be unleashed...*

The intruder doesn't move an inch. The leader decides to call out the sick man's name.

"John! Talk to me! What's going on??"

*John?*

*John.*

More groans, which rapidly escalate to screams. Suddenly the Native American man breaks his stance and turns, one more time, in an attempt to attend to the sick man. Fed by raw impulse and the sudden amount of pressure, the leader pulls the trigger.

A clean, dry BANG.

Abrupt silence overtakes the desert. The groans have stopped. Smoke and gun powder clouds the armed man's vision. He breathes heavily. His blood-pumping heart beats loudly, deep inside his ears. He squints, unable to see, but never lowers his weapon.

"John?"

Then he finally sees it. As the curtain of smoke clears, John, the young man, stands opposite him; the Native American lies crouched on the ground behind him, out of harm's way.

A perforation is evident on John's chest, but no blood. He looks down at it, confused. Suddenly a stream of blue light jets out of the bullet hole blinding the leader momentarily. He takes a few steps back, trips and lands on his injured spine. He lets out a stymied sob.

More streams radiate out of John's chest and spiral around him, weaving into a sphere of light. The blue beams pulsate, contracting in and out, spiraling and interweaving organically.

Sharp, crystalline needles, shoot out of the light sphere and sink back in. The motion repeats as the sphere reaches a stage of maximum incandescence.

The exquisite aurora blinds the leader. Then it happens. He sees it all. Propelled by an exterior force, his eyes snap wide open, enveloped by the radiant white.

Snippets of the entire universe flash before his mind's eye. Past. Present. Future. All possibilities flicker past his very own eyes in a moment of transcendence. Before he can grasp any sense of what's happening, the sphere contracts to the size of a marble and vanishes completely.

Overwhelmed and drained of color, the leader faints, collapsing onto the dirt.

The leader rises, rubbing his eyes. Stars have fully faded, as blue and yellow morning hues take over the deep blacks of the night.

He looks around, confused: *what in the world happened?*

The fire has long been extinguished; only ashes remain.

Both the Native American man and John are missing. No trace of them left behind, except for the intruder's bowl. He picks it up and sniffs its contents. He frowns and takes a sip. The deeply furrowed brow immediately softens, as he pours the rest of the contents into his parched mouth— every last drop in desperation.

*Water.*

He reaches the top of a tall cliff, sits down on a large rock, and admires the vast view. The sun rises, breaking through the irregular horizon line created by the silhouetted mountains, laying out a blanket of pink and orange. Not a cloud in sight.

He takes a deep breath, taking it all in, enjoying the beginning of a new day, sensing creatures throughout the globe groggily rising, preparing to face this clean slate of possibilities.

He retrieves his diary and begins to write.

## *This has happened before.*

I'm back in my room. With Nina.

We are covered in purple and green. The neon lights from the convenience store next door bleed in through the blinds on my bedroom window. She wraps around me, or under me, or next to me, not sure where's up and where's down—she becomes an extension of myself.

# R³

I get lost in her eyes—so many different colors and shapes, constantly moving and shifting like tectonic plates—true kaleidoscope eyes reeling me into an unknown world, a great whirlpool of fate sucking me in.

My entire body vibrates. A strange electric current grips my muscles as she kisses my neck gently. Electrons spark whenever our skins touch. There is no pain; only pleasure. Skin on skin contact is purely orgasmic.

"You know what you have to do," she says into my ear.

I nod, not knowing what she's talking about. Suddenly my entire body contracts, jerking my jaw open as a violent gasp scrapes my dry throat. Sweat pours profusely out of my every pore as my eyes are forced wide open, and all I see is her; Nina, glowing on top of me.

She guides my hands, wrapping them around her elegant neck.

"You must live," she says.

These words resonate in my mind as I fight every urge to strangle Nina. My entire being is suddenly controlled by an external force, a force trying to terminate her.

Every muscle in my body tenses, my face boils red, fighting the external force. A painful groan parts my clenched teeth as I begin to release Nina's neck from my grasp—the bones in my fingers and hands cracking and snapping—and I pull my hands down towards my own neck. Once there, they lock and I gasp.

# R³

The shiny metallic object moves fast.

Fast.

FAST.

Cutting through the vibrant, space-like environment, leaving massive diamond-shaped ripples behind.

Isaac lies dead on the floor.

Back in my apartment.

The hammer incident with Dr. Hammond has just occurred.

Suddenly his blood seeps back into his body. Reawakened, he jolts back to life, every movement in reverse motion, rewinding like a tape back to before Isaac's death.

And there he is. Alive, standing in front of me, his back turned to me, his eyes glued to the coffee table in the middle of the room. The R³ bottle, the pharmaceutical bottles, the old syringe—the buffet of drugs, all laid out. On perfect display.

From behind, Isaac slowly reaches towards his waistcoat: *a gun?* Cold sweat trickles down my neck and spine. It has to be a gun. My eyes dart around the room, looking for something.

*This has happened before.*

# R³

There's no time. Isaac turns briskly, his hand wrapped around a cold, black object.

The metallic projectile pierces through the air, travelling at super speed, surrounded by colorful streaks, seconds away from reaching its target.

When it finally cuts through a chromatic membrane—the "hole in the stratosphere"—our surroundings become hazy.

And far below we see the city... getting closer and closer...

*Everything falls, everything lands, everything arrives at its destination and comes full circle.*

Isaac holds the black object—his phone—against his ear. It rings. My eyes dart to the table where the hammer should've been, except it's not. It's not there.

The hammer isn't there.

The hammer wasn't there.

Dr. Hammond's hammer was never there.

"You're fucked, Hammond," Isaac sneers. "Fucked."

I can hear the 911 operator faintly on the other end of the receiver.

# R³

And then it happens.

I hear the window glass *pop* seconds before the sixteenth century rifle bullet pierces through my chest.

It's finally reached me.

Blood sputters out. I look down, confused, corking the opening with my hand.

My knees fail, allowing my body to cave in, victim to gravity.

*Everything falls…*

Isaac doesn't move. Panic takes over his now fragile body. He lowers the phone and looks around, hoping to find the reset button. But it isn't there. This is the reset. *He looks so small,* I think, *so helpless.*

"I didn't shoot. I didn't shoot!" he screams to no one, to the neighbors, to god, maybe to himself—who knows—, as my face distorts in pain and I finally collapse on the floor.

Dead.

Isaac looks around, lost.

## *Time to become one again.*

I'm back in my apartment. All my furniture remains pushed up against the door and windows, barricading every exit.

I sit in the middle of the room as blue-ish light beams out of my mouth and eyes. The bloody bandages remain on the rippling floor below me. The membrane on the top of my head glows faintly.

That's when I feel it. The string pulling me back in. Pulling us all back together, one by one. My wondering eyes look down, finding a hole—a bullet hole—on my chest. It doesn't bleed blood, but it bleeds light, a blue light.

Slightly curious, I stick my finger into the orifice and slowly pull it open. There's no discernible pain or discomfort.

The exposed insides of my body reveal themselves to be bright blue crystal beads in myriad shapes and sizes, arranged inside me in no particular fashion. The light pulsates like a beating heart.

The front door is pushed open, moving furniture aside, but I care too little to turn and see who it is.

The intruder makes his way up to me, walks around, and finally faces me. I look up with clouded eyes, coming face to face with my kaleidoscopic self.

With John.

My other self who woke up in the incubator, finally freed from hypnosis.

He knows it's time…

Time to become one again.

In sync with one another, he crouches and sticks his head into the opening in my chest. His arms and torso follow. The bright blue crystals absorb the rest of his body with welcoming ease.

Suddenly the light increases to a blinding level, consuming everything in sight. Then back to darkness.

The apartment is now empty. We are both gone.

The dirty bandages remain on the floor.

Abandoned. Forgotten. Alone

*March 14ᵗʰ, 1592*

    *It was gone, as fast as it'd appeared. No longer to be seen, devoured by the void. It was everything and anything all at once. It was beautiful. I saw it all, the end through the beginning. As a mathematician, my initial reaction was to examine, to deconstruct, but even as numbers, the knowledge*

# R³

*was ungraspable. I was ecstatic, filled with joy as tears swelled my eyes. Yet all I did was smile. It was the absolute. The first and the last. Infinity within the water drop. All infinite potentials and outcomes in one.*

*Nothing in my life had ever prepared me for this experience. Millions of thoughts flooded my mind, instantly doubting what my every sense was experiencing. I blamed it on my lack of water; dehydrated for days. The scorching sun overpowered my weak limbs, but I knew I had a grip on my wits. This was real. Real as real can get. Tangible as tangible gets. It wasn't my tired mind playing tricks on me because I was not the only one there. Yet, I was the only one left. The thought of poison did cross my mind. A strong hallucinogen, perhaps? But I hadn't ingested anything other than what was in my pack. Another disproving option, discarded. What struck me the most, however, was what followed.*

*A sequence of infinite numbers flashed before me. Then merged into one. Next, lives flickered past me. They also merged into one. Past, present, future; all radiated through the one eye, the source. And that's when I knew—this was the answer.*

*The answer to everything, to every single question. The secret to all life and the universe.*

# $R^3$

*We are all born to d—*

## NON-SPACE & NON-TIME ENVIRONMENT

Lights flash everywhere around us on a black canvas, as if we were traveling through space, except we are aware that this is not "space". Various coruscations of light and images pass us, some resembling aurora borealis, others pixels and phosphorescent geometry.

Our movement slows down as we reach a giant,

# R³

glowing triangle—the entrance to a tunnel. It's lit from within. We're inside it. Mystified as we are, we are not scared.

The tunnel becomes a cube, not too big, not too small. Grooves cover its every surface forming spatially pleasant patterns. The intricacy and attention to detail is reminiscent of ancient hieroglyphs. Streams of light pulsate along the wall's crevices, up and down, left to right, bursting like shooting stars constrained to a secure track. They outline every single pattern, before fading away completely.

We face something that wasn't there before and float towards it, self-propelled through the vacuous air.

Facing us is a sphere of glass-like light. Pulsating crystal spikes undulate in and out, constantly in motion, breathing—both exceptionally beautiful and soothing.

We approach, confident. Our faces reflect back at us on the glass-like surface. Millions of tiny "Johns" all over. Our facial features gradually blur out, leaving only a peach-colored dot on the reflection.

Blank.

Smooth skin, revealing no signs of expression, bone structure or breathing orifices.

Suddenly a gust of wind materializes out of nowhere and blows little, crystal pieces off our bodies. We quickly realize, these crystal particles are in fact ourselves—we are disintegrating.

# R³

In a matter of seconds, our entire being has broken down into tiny, twinkling flecks that descend as if pulled by some foreign source of gravity.

When examined up close, the crystal-like particles are in fact: snowflakes. All of them unique. None of them alike. As they fall, they sparkle vibrantly, cascading down toward a vast pool of water below us that seems to extend to infinity—water and sky merging at the horizon.

The pool mirrors the shimmering snowflakes as they finally land on its surface, melting, fusing completely with the water.

The snowflakes fully dissolve into the ocean. A faint glimmer glows on its surface, but soon fades away.

As we descend and transition through the liquid, the emptiness surrounding us gradually takes shape, becoming red and warm. A single object morphs before us, shifting into a small, round head.

We float in the plasmatic liquid, next to an unborn child. Curious, we swim around it, hoping to get a full view of its face.

The unborn child has one eye. It sits somewhere between where both eyes should normally be.

Suddenly it snaps open. The iris is partially dilated, revealing kaleidoscopic patterns. Its gaze is fixated on us.

Blink. And we switch.

# R³

It's us, staring out, waiting silently, taking the baby's point of view, gazing at the vacuity of our unfamiliar, yet alluring, surroundings.

We can feel its serenity…

…which gradually becomes ours.

We can hear its heartbeat…

…which gradually becomes ours.

And then we hear her voice:

…*dream.*

Yet we soon wake up and forget.